Splitting Issues

(And Several Other Noteworthy Concerns)

A Bunch of Short Plays

by

Sam Bobrick

SAMUEL FRENCH

FOUNDED 1830

NEW YORK HOLLYWOOD LONDON TORONTO

SAMUELFRENCH.COM

ISBN 978-0-573-66268-3   Printed in U.S.A.   #20877

IMPORTANT BILLING AND CREDIT REQUIREMENTS

CHARACTERS

This play can be done with as few as six actors - 3 men, 3 women

ACT I

SPLITTING ISSUES
PETE – early thirties
GWEN – same
LARRY – same
MARCIE – same

DO YOU COME HERE OFTEN?
BOB – late thirties
NAN – late thirties

PURGATORY
JACK – early forties
RICHARD – same

MAY I RECOMMEND THE CROW?
JOYCE – late-forties
CHARLES – same

ACT II

CLEARING THE AIR
CLARK – late twenties, early-thirties
JILL – same
EMMA – same
HARRISON – same

BINGO–BANGO
FRED – mid-thirties
ROSALIND – same
ZOE – same
IAN – same

DINNER WITH FRIENDLY NEIGHBORS
DONNA – early thirties
NICK – same
IRENE – early fifties
WAYNE – same

HOLLYWOOD LOVE STORY
ALAN – mid-thirties
KAREN – same
DAVID – late forties
TRISH – early thirties

THE FAILURE
WILLIAM – early fifties
VICTORIA – same

SETS

The play, which consists of nine sketches, can be done with a minimum of sets, i.e. chairs, a sofa, benches, etc. and a background curtain.

ACT I

Scene 1

SPLITTING ISSUES

TIME: The present. An early spring evening.

PLACE: The living room of Gwen and Pete Darren, a couple in their early thirties. At Center Stage is a love seat flanked by two side chairs. A coffee table is in front of the love seat. There is a small table at Stage Right, near the entrance to the apartment which is Off Stage Right. Several feet behind the love seat are two flats. In between them is the entrance to the kitchen. The necessary props, dishes, wine glasses, etc., can be on a small table in the kitchen area.

AT RISE: GWEN *ENTERS from the kitchen with some napkins and plates and places them on the coffee table. A few beats later* PETE *ENTERS from the kitchen with four wine glasses and sets them down. The two are very matter of fact with each other.*

PETE. Do they know it's not for dinner?

GWEN. I didn't mention dinner when I invited them over.

PETE. Then they know it's just for wine and cheese.

GWEN. I think so.

PETE. *(Worried)* You think so?

GWEN. Well, you have to understand I was upset at the time. But I think…No, I'm actually certain I told them just wine and cheese.

PETE. What about dip?

GWEN. I didn't mention dip.

PETE. But we have dip?

GWEN. Yes, but I'm not going to offer it because I think wine and cheese will be enough.

PETE. Not if they're expecting dinner.

GWEN. For the last time, I did not mention dinner.

PETE. Yes, but that doesn't mean they're not expecting it. I think it's the time you asked them to come over that's bugging me. You don't ask people to come by at seven unless it's for dinner.

GWEN. Oh, God. Are you going to be on me all night about this?

(She EXITS to kitchen)

PETE. No. It's just that, well, it's such a sticky situation. I don't want to make it any more difficult than it's going to be and if they come over expecting dinner and not getting it, well, that's just going to add to the stress of the evening. What kind did you get?

GWEN. *(ENTERS with cheese platter)* What kind of what did I get?

PETE. Cheese? What kind of cheese did you get?

GWEN. The usual. Brie and cheddar.

PETE. Just two kinds?

GWEN. Yes. I believe Brie and cheddar are just two kinds.

(She sets the platter down on the coffee table)

PETE. Too bad. It's good to have choices.

GWEN. *(She is clearly losing patience)* We *have* choices. Brie or cheddar. Now will you lay off.

(She begins positioning the chairs so they'll be just right)

PETE. Okay. Okay. I don't mean to upset you.

GWEN. Sometimes I think you do.

PETE. Well, I don't.

(A beat)

But you should think about the dip just in case.

GWEN. *(Defiant)* I will *never* think about the dip.

PETE. *(A beat)* Okay, okay. Don't think about it.

GWEN. I won't.

PETE. Just keep it in the back of your mind. That's not thinking about it. That's just storing it. Should I open the wine now?

GWEN. If you want.

PETE. Red or white?

GWEN. I'll let you make the call.

PETE. I'll open the white. It's cheaper.

GWEN. What if they want red?

PETE. Then I'll open the red.

(Pete EXITS into kitchen)

GWEN. And what will you do with the white?

PETE *(O.S.)* *I'll* drink it.

GWEN. You don't like white.

PETE. *(ENTERS with a bottle of white wine and a cork screw and begins opening it)*
I'll mix it with the red. It'll be a Rosé. I don't mind Rosé. What about crackers?

GWEN. I'm getting them.

(She EXITS into kitchen)

PETE. Did you get the little wheat ones I like?

GWEN *(O.S.)* No.

PETE. Why not?

GWEN. Because you like them.

PETE. I understand.

(Gwen ENTERS with plate of crackers)

Boy, I'll bet they're going to be surprised why we're having them over.

GWEN. I'm sure they will be.

PETE. I'm sort of surprised too. I mean, I expected it, but then, I didn't really expect it. Do you know what I mean?

GWEN. Not at all.

PETE. Well, no sense trying to explain it. It's all water under the bridge now, isn't it?

GWEN. It certainly is.

PETE. You know I never knew what that meant. Water under the bridge. I've used it a lot but I never did get it, did you? I never got that or "beyond the pale." That's another one I didn't get.

GWEN. Look, are you trying to make conversation?

PETE. Yes.

GWEN. Don't. The less we have to say to one another, the better. After this is over I never want to talk to you or see you ever again.

PETE. Fine, fine. That's okay with me. Whatever you want.

GWEN. That's what I want.

PETE. Well, then that's what I want too. Besides the dip.

GWEN. Oh, Christ.

PETE. Do me a favor. Bring out the dip. It would just make me feel better. It's the last thing I will ever ask you to do. I promise. Please?

GWEN. *(Fed up)* Okay, okay. I'll get the dip. I'll get the goddamn dip.

PETE. That's my girl.

GWEN. Not any more.

PETE. I know. I'm well aware of that. It's just an expression I used in happier times. I'm sure I'll grow accustomed to not using it.

GWEN. Good. And the sooner the better.

(She EXITS to kitchen)

PETE. Okay, okay. I hope you're not getting angry? I'd really hate for them to see you angry. It's not very becoming. Besides, we decided to handle this like adults. I know I will. I think I've been doing a good job so far. The key word should be "reasonable." For the most part I've always been a reasonable person, even you have to admit that. Sure, sometimes I'll slam a door or kick the wall in or throw a vase at a mirror when I'm upset, but when a couple is no longer speaking to one another, there aren't very many other ways to communicate displeasure. Besides I haven't done anything like that for days, which in my opinion clearly shows a great degree of growth, restraint and fiscal responsibility. I'm a patient man who is willing to go down new avenues, take on new adventures, while you unfortunately don't have the open-mindedness to implement and appreciate the necessary actions needed to institute any degree of behavior change. No, you unfortunately are the kind who would rather curse the darkness than light one small candle.

GWEN. *(Gwen ENTERS with a bowl of dip and stares at him for a beat)* Will you shut the fuck up!

PETE. Sorry. I didn't know you were listening.

GWEN. *(Shoves the bowl into his chest)* Here's your stupid dip.

PETE. *(Places dip on coffee table)* Thank you. Trust me, it's going to make the evening a much bigger success. There's no worse feeling than having guests over and sending them home unsatisfied. One thing about dip, it's a universal satisfier. You eat it and you almost don't care to eat anything else. It's kind of an appetite ruiner, which isn't bad when you're not getting dinner. What kind is it?

GWEN. It's onion!

PETE. Onion?

GWEN. Onion!

PETE. What if they don't like onion?

GWEN. Then I will dump the bowl of dip on your head.

PETE. Okay. Fair enough.

(Looks at watch)

It's after seven. I hope nothing's happened to them. Do you think we should put on some CD's? Have a little background music?

GWEN. Look, get this through your head. This is not a party. You and I are divorcing, splitting up, calling it a day. What kind of music could possibly go with that?

PETE. Country and Western?

GWEN. *(Takes a deep breath)* What did I ever see in you?

PETE. Nothing. You just thought it was time to get married. I think we had this discussion before.

(SOUND: DOORBELL)

That's them. I'll get it. Let's hope they're not expecting dinner.

(Pete EXITS off stage to front door)

PETE *(O.S.) (CONTINUED)* Larry! Marcie! Come on in.

LARRY *(O.S.)* Hey, Pete.

MARCIE *(O.S.)* Hi, Pete.

*(Pete ENTERS room with **MARCIE** and **LARRY**, also in their early thirties. They have flowers and a box of candy. They greet Gwen with a hug.)*

MARCIE *(CONTINUED)* Gwen.

LARRY. Hey, Gwen.

GWEN. Hello, Marcie. Hello. Larry. Glad you could make it.

(Indicating flowers and candy in Larry's hand)

Are those for us?

MARCIE. Well, yes and no. We weren't sure about tonight's invitation. If its for dinner, then they're both for you. If it's just for wine and cheese, then I'd like to take the box of candy back home with us. We're invited over to another couples next week who are serving dinner and I can bring the candy to them.

PETE. It's just for wine and cheese.

MARCIE. That's fine. We'll just leave the candy by the door.

PETE. But we're also having dip.

LARRY. Dip doesn't count. The candy goes home.

(Larry puts the candy on a nearby table and Marcie hands the flowers to Gwen)

GWEN. Oh, carnations. My favorite.

MARCIE. I thought they must be. You always bring them to us. I never really cared for them, but I figured you did.

LARRY. You guys have us all excited. Just what was it that had to be discussed so immediately and so urgently?

PETE. Well, maybe you'd better sit down for this.

GWEN. Offer them some wine first, Pete.

PETE. Wine! Right. How about a nice glass of white?

MARCIE & LARRY. Red!

PETE. Damn! Be right back.

(Starts towards kitchen)

GWEN. Bring a vase for the flowers.

PETE. Right.

(Pete EXITS to kitchen. Marcie sits down on the sofa and helps herself to the cheese and crackers)

MARCIE. You're expecting, aren't you? That's what I told Larry it was. You're expecting and we are the first to know.

GWEN. No, we're divorcing and you're the first to know.

(Only Larry's reaction is big. Marcie seems not to be that shaken by the news)

LARRY. What?

GWEN. That's right. Divorcing. Splitting up. Calling it a day. Finished, dead, done!

LARRY. I can't believe it. When did this all come about?

(Pete ENTERS with a bottle of red wine, a corkscrew and an empty vase. During the following Gwen takes the vase, puts the flowers in them and sets them on the table next to the box of candy)

PETE. This morning at breakfast. I asked her to pass the goddamn toast and she asked me to move out of the goddamn house.

MARCIE. *(Bites into the cheese and cracker)* Oh, my God. This

Brie is fabulous. Try some Larry.

LARRY. Sure. I'm starved. We haven't had dinner yet.

(Sits next to Marcie and helps himself to the cheese and crackers)

GWEN. We're trying to go about this in a very mature and civil way so there won't be any problems down the line.

PETE. We've already settled on splitting up the furniture, what I'm going to get, what she's going to get. Now we need to split up our friends.

MARCIE. Really? That's so cute.

PETE. See, one thing that happens when a couple splits up, some of their friends stay friends with the husband…

GWEN. …and some of their friends stay friends with the wife.

LARRY. Well, you don't have to worry about us. We think the world of you two and we will remain friends with both of you.

PETE. Yes, but well, that's not what we want. Our issues are so vast and bitter that we never want to see or hear from each other ever again.

(To Gwen)

Right, sweetheart?

(Catches himself)

I'm sorry. Scratch "sweetheart." Just another habit that I'm going to need to break.

GWEN. My dislike for this man is so great, that as far as I'm concerned, any friend of Pete's can never be a friend of mine.

PETE. And vice-versa of course.

MARCIE. It's a bit extreme, isn't it?

GWEN. Yes, but actually the idea of splitting up our friends is one of the few things we've agreed on since we've been married. Anyway, we've invited you here to let you choose which one of us you want to remain friends with.

LARRY. This is so crazy. We never would have expected anything like this in a million years. What the hell happened between you two?

PETE. It's not important.

LARRY. Of course it is.

GWEN. It would just open old wounds.

LARRY. It doesn't matter. We'd like to know the problem. Maybe we can help fix it.

PETE. It seems to have gone beyond fixing.

GWEN. Our marriage was a big mistake.

PETE. We had too many issues that couldn't be worked out.

GWEN. It started with decorating the apartment.

PETE. She wanted Pottery Barn. I wanted Crate and Barrel.

MARCIE. Aren't they basically the same crap?

GWEN. Not to the discerning eye. From there it progressed to bigger things. What to watch on TV, what kind of car to buy, what to name the cat…

PETE. I wanted to call it Max. She wanted to call it Lorraine after her mother.

LARRY. I didn't know you had a cat.

PETE. We don't. Who in their right mind would want to bring an animal into this unhappy household?

MARCIE. Have you been to a marriage counselor?

GWEN. We've been to several.

PETE. Six.

MARCIE. And?

PETE. Five of them thought we should divorce and the sixth, well it was really hard to get a good reading. Half-way through the session she threw us out of her office.

GWEN. That was your fault. You threw a vase at her mirror.

PETE. Well, she got me mad. She had no business telling me I was behaving like a baby.

GWEN. Anyway, we would like to give you two the opportunity to decide who you want to remain friendly with.

PETE. And we've both agreed that who ever you pick, whether it's Gwen or myself, the other will understand and there'll be no hard feelings.

MARCIE. *(Biting into a cheese and cracker)* This is unbelievable. Absolutely unbelievable. The Brie. Where did you get it?

GWEN. There's a little cheese shop around the corner.

MARCIE. *(To Larry)* As soon as we leave, Larry, and if it's still open, we've got to pick some up. With a better wine this would be heaven.

PETE. What's wrong with the wine?

MARCIE. Nothing. It's fine. But like everything in life there's fine and there's better.

GWEN. Forget the wine, forget the cheese. I'm dying to know which one of us you guys will choose.

PETE. So would I? Actually Gwen and I have a bet on it.

MARCIE. That's sick.

(Until her next speech, Marcie doesn't seem that interested in the conversation)

PETE. I know. That's another reason we need to split. We're obviously not a very healthy pair.

GWEN. Come on. Pick.

PETE. And incidentally, you don't have to do it as a couple. You can do it individually.

GWEN. You know, it just dawned on me that this would make a wonderful reality TV show.

PETE. It would, wouldn't it? We should look into this?

GWEN. What do you mean, we? It was my idea.

PETE. We're still married. It's community property.

GWEN. You are such a pig.

PETE. I just want to be fair to myself. What's wrong with that?

GWEN. *(To the others)* We'd better rush it before he starts throwing things.

LARRY. No, this is just too crazy and too quick for us to digest. Think about it. You two are splitting up. If there was one marriage in our crowd that I had to bet on, it would be yours. It's an absolute shock. In fact, it's quite threatening. You know we love you both.

PETE. Come on, come on. No copping out. This is a moment of truth.

LARRY. I know, I know. This really puts us in an awkward position…

PETE. Do you think a little mood music would help? At the car wash this morning, for only three ninety-nine I picked up the sound track from "Schindler's List."

LARRY. No, no, that's okay. I seem to be drifting towards a decision. If I had to make a choice…which of you I will remain friends with…

GWEN & PETE. Yes?

LARRY. It will be…

GWEN & PETE. Yes?

LARRY. I'm going to pick…

(Points to Gwen)

You!

PETE. *(Surprised)* Gwen!

GWEN. *(Excited. Like a TV game show winner)* Me! I knew it. I knew it. I'm so happy. I really am. This has made my day.

(To Pete)

See, you smug bastard. I told you he liked me better. And this is your best friend, so now you should realize more than ever, what a worthless piece of garbage you are.

PETE. I'm hurt, Larry. I'm really hurt.

LARRY. Look, I did not do this willy-nilly. A lot of thought went into my decision.

PETE. What kind of thought? You've been here five minutes.

LARRY. I just feel Gwen will need more support than you will. Let's face it. It's still a man's world. The fact is, we can get women anytime we want, but a divorced chick, well, it's a different story. Especially one in her thirties.

GWEN. God. I just went from feeling like a winner to feeling like a total loser.

LARRY. Come on. Let's be honest. No matter how we all try to be politically correct, you have to be a realist. Once you two split, Gwen is going to need all the people around her she can get and well, I feel as a friend to both of you, I'd be doing the right thing to be there for her.

GWEN. God, what a wonderful person you turned out to be, Larry.

LARRY. I know.

PETE. Bullshit, Larry. Bullshit! Bullshit! Bullshit! You're not fooling me one bit. I know your game, you scumbag. You're figuring once I'm out of the picture you're finally going to be able to nail her, which is what I felt you wanted to do from the very day you met her.

GWEN. Really, Larry. I'm flattered.

PETE. Hey, don't think I don't know how a guy thinks. You know she'll be alone. You'll commiserate with her problems. Show concern. You'll meet for lunch. You'll have drinks. You'll be sympathetic. Act like the big brother. One drink leads to a second. The next thing you know you'll be over here in my bed screwing her brains out.

GWEN. That is vile. That is so vile. First of all, if you remember, we divided up the furniture and I got the bed. So for all practical purposes it's my bed, not your bed.

PETE. It is? What did I pick?

GWEN. The refrigerator.

PETE. I'm still happy with my choice.

MARCIE. (*Finally getting involved*) Boy, oh, boy, oh boy. You have to hand it to Pete, Larry. He sure has you pegged.

PETE. I do?

MARCIE. You bet that dick is going to try to screw Gwen. That's exactly what he did when Ty and Denise split up.

PETE. You had an affair with Denise?

LARRY. It wasn't an affair. She was lonely. I met her for lunch. One drink led to another and the next thing I knew...

MARCIE. He was in her bedroom screwing her brains out.

LARRY. Okay, okay. But before you draw any conclusions, I just want you to know that I'm probably more responsible for bringing those two back together than anyone.

GWEN. How was that?

MARCIE. Bad sex.

LARRY. It wasn't that bad, trust me. She just realized how much more carnally comfortable she was with Ty. Those two did some kinky things. I tried to be as accommodating as I could, but there are certain things in bed even I won't do.

MARCIE. I know. I have my own list.

LARRY. There was just too much leather involved. I still have marks on my back from the whip. Anyway, it all worked out because as soon as Denise realized how much more compatible she was with Ty, she went back with him and I felt wonderful that I was able to contribute to that.

GWEN. You know, Larry, you really are a nice guy, aren't you?

PETE. Nice, my ass. That was a horrendous story. That was betrayal on every level. How the hell can you be so blasé about it? And you, Marcie, you had to be shattered.

MARCIE. I didn't find out till after it was over. I put two and two together when, out of gratitude, they sent Larry a fruit basket.

LARRY. I thought it was very nice of them. We had

grapefruits for three weeks.

MARCIE. Yes, but the plums were all squishy. I love fruit. By any chance, you don't happen to have any? It goes quite well with Brie.

GWEN. No. No fruit. Just wine, cheese and dip.

MARCIE. Pity.

PETE. Oh, come on, Marcie. Larry's affair had to affect your relationship with him. I mean you had to be angry.

MARCIE. Well, rather than get mad, I thought it was more important to our relationship that I got even.

LARRY. And did she ever. She had an affair with Denise too. Wild chick that Denise. Anyway, it took the edge off of what could have been a very sticky situation and we've managed to remain great friends with them.

PETE. God, that is a sick and depraved story.

LARRY. Yeah, but I've checked around and it's not that uncommon in today's complicated, but broad minded world.

GWEN. Well, at least Ty and Denise's story had a happy ending. It's obvious Pete's and mine won't.

PETE. What's more disappointing is you, Larry. Choosing Gwen over me. We've been friends since high school. I know if you and Marcie were splitting up and I had to make a choice of who's friend I'd be, so help me, without a moments of hesitation, I would choose you.

LARRY. I think you're starting to take this a little too personal.

PETE. Of course I am, damn it. In the back of my mind, I always suspected I was a better friend to you than you were to me. How right I was. I'm going to need to do some heavy duty rethinking about our friendship.

GWEN. Why? You probably won't see him again. He just chose me over you, remember? Besides, that's the way some relationships are. Sometimes one person likes another person much better than the other person likes that person. You may have considered Larry your best friend, but maybe he never considered you his best friend.

PETE. Could that possibly be true, Larry?

LARRY. I really don't think it's necessary to go there, Pete.

PETE. Oh, my God, it is true. I'm not your best friend.

LARRY. Look, Pete, I like you a lot. I really do. I enjoy having a meal with you now and then, watching a football game or two a year with you, but look, I need to be honest. As far as your being my very, very best friend, well…I'm sorry.

PETE. I'm crushed. I'm friggen crushed…It's Arnie Tucker, isn't it? I should have known it was Arnie. The way you two slow danced together New Years Eve, that should have been the tip off.

LARRY. I admit Arnie and I had a little too much to drink that night, but it isn't Arnie.

PETE. I'm really disappointed in you Larry.

GWEN. God, Pete, you sound like a jilted lover.

PETE. This evening has turned into a nightmare. Losing my wife and now finding out I don't have a best friend. There's a sense of security lost here. A sense that when the chips are down, there would always be someone there for me. And now I realize there's not. I feel so alone. So naked. So unprotected.

MARCIE. I love this Brie.

LARRY. Look, cheer up, Pete. It's not over yet. Marcie has yet to make a choice of who she wants to remain friends with. There's still a chance it could be you.

PETE. Yes. That's true.

GWEN. Larry's right, Pete. Don't give up hope yet, although I think it stands to reason if Larry's going to be friends with me, it would just make it easier for Marcie to go along with that.

PETE. Is that true, Marcie?

MARCIE. Well, since it seems we're all being a little too honest for our own good, I'd like to take the opportunity to go with my true feelings and choose neither of you.

GWEN. Really?

MARCIE. Look, Larry and Pete were friends before I entered the picture. When I married Larry, his friends became my friends. Frankly, I don't feel that close to either one of you. Not that I dislike you. I'm just not all that enthused about being around you. Truthfully, if I was never to see either of you again, as far as I'm concerned, it would just be water under the bridge.

PETE. Ahh, so that's what it means.

GWEN. God, Marcie, I have been so nice to you. When you and Larry got married, I insisted we send you three place settings of your dishes. Pete wanted to send you the George Foreman grill.

PETE. I thought Larry would have liked it better.

GWEN. But I knew Marcie wouldn't have. I was thinking of her. And now when my world is falling apart and I need all the comforting I can get, she decides to be totally honest with me. That is the most insensitive thing I have had to deal with in a long, long time. I think I'm going to cry.

(Begins weeping softly)

PETE. Now look what you did. I hate when she cries.

MARCIE. I'm sorry. I saw a window of opportunity and I took it.

PETE. (Trying to console Gwen) Try to pull yourself together, honey. Forget about what Marcie just said. Try to think of some good things. Some positive things.

GWEN. (Sniffles) Like what?

PETE. Well, like getting rid of me.

GWEN. (Stops the crying) Yes, that's true. That does help a little.

PETE. Good.

MARCIE. Look, maybe it'll make things easier if I explain myself a little further. I am a product of a very privileged background. Private schools, family money, a distrust of humor…I really have very little in common with you two. At best, you're a simple, middle class couple totally without style or taste. Just as an example of what I mean by that, you invited us here for wine and cheese. Well then serve wnie and cheese and go with it. For Chris sake, you didn't have to put out an onion dip. I mean, how trailer trash is that?

GWEN. Well, since you're being so goddamn honest with me, Marcie, let me be goddamn honest with you. Don't think for one minute I didn't notice you turning your nose up at everything I do or have, my cooking, my clothes, our dishes, our silverware…

MARCIE. Silver-plate! You don't have silverware darling, you have silver-plate. It's one fourth the cost.

PETE. Really? Damn, I picked that over the bookcase.

GWEN. You are an absolute phony, Marcie. There is not one genuine bone in your body. Everything about you, is about status. The stores you go to, the stupid logos on all your clothes, to let people know you spent twice as much as you had to for the ugliest crap I've ever seen. Real money, real class doesn't have to go that route. And I'll tell you something else. The cheddar is a much better cheese than the Brie, but because Brie is a French word, you choose to like it better. But here's the good news about Brie. It's got three times the fat as Cheddar and I hope it clogs your arteries and you die.

LARRY. Excuse me, but I think we're really drifting into girl talk now. I have a wonderful idea. Let's send out for Chinese. Pete and Gwen pay and we can leave the candy here.

PETE. No, forget it. Gwen and I thought we had friends. It's obvious we don't. I don't want to ever see you two slime balls again.

LARRY. Oh, come on. You can't mean that?

PETE. You're damn right, I do. I don't care how badly Gwen

and I treat each other, we're man and wife and that's our privilege. But I do care how others treat us. You people are crazy, insensitive jerks and we will do very well without you in our lives. This evening has made me realize something very important.

GWEN. Like what, Pete?

PETE. That when your ass is on the line, you can never count on good friends to be good friends. That's why Gwen, when you pick your next husband, you make sure he's someone who will stand by you, take your side, be your pal through thick and thin.

GWEN. Just the way you're doing now.

PETE. Exactly.

(To Marcie and Larry)

As for you two, you can take your candy and just get the hell out of our lives.

MARCIE. Fine. Fine with me. Come on, Larry.

(She swallows down one more piece of Brie and rises)

LARRY. *(Taking the candy)* Shall I take the flowers too?

(Lifts the flowers from the vase)

PETE. *(Grabbing the flowers from Larry)* Over my dead body. These flowers are for my wife.

LARRY. Okay, okay.

(To Marcie)

Let's go, honey. This is a very troubled couple.

MARCIE. Listen, it's still early. Why don't we stop over at Ty and Denise's and see what they're doing.

LARRY. Good idea.

(They EXIT. Pete and Gwen stare after them for a beat. Pete then turns to Gwen and hands her the flowers)

PETE. For you.

GWEN. Thank you. It was wonderful the way you stood up for me.

PETE. Well, I'm still your husband.

GWEN. Yes, you are. And it was quite wonderful and I really didn't expect it. You turned out to be a very caring person after all.

PETE. I love you Gwen. I love you very much. We need to try again.

GWEN. No. No, I'm sorry but that's not possible, Pete.

PETE. Why not?

GWEN. Because as long as I live, I will *never, ever* forgive you for making me put out the onion dip. I'd like you out by Thursday.

PETE. No problem. You want to pour a glass of red wine for me?

GWEN. Sure. Shall I mix it with some white.

PETE. Good idea.

(They sit down around the cheese as the LIGHTS DIM)

End of Act I, Scene 1

ACT I

Scene 2

DO YOU COME HERE OFTEN?

TIME: *The present. Evening.*

PLACE: *A Ballroom.*

MUSIC: SOFT DANCE MUSIC IN BG that slowly FADES OUT.

AT RISE: **NAN** *and* **BOB**, *both in their late thirties, are seated on individual chairs a few feet away from one another, staring out into the audience, watching make believe dancers, yet still giving the audience a feeling that they're both waiting for something. Bob is wearing a very loud sport coat, colored shirt and tie. Nan is wearing a dress a little too flashy for a singles dance. Although they are obviously not together, every now and then, one looks at the other and smiles. Bob finally moves his chair close to Nan.*

BOB. My name's Bob.

NAN. I'm Nan.

BOB. Hi, Nan.

NAN. Hi, Bob.

BOB. *(A beat. Uneasy)* Hi, Nan.

NAN. Hi, Bob.

(Another beat)

BOB. Hi, Nan.

NAN. Hi, Bob.

(They both laugh. The ice has been broken)

BOB. Do you come here often?

NAN. No, not really.

BOB. Me neither.

NAN. Maybe once a week.

BOB. Yeah, me too. About once a week.

(A beat. And then in desperation to keep the conversation going.)

NAN. Usually Friday nights.

BOB. Yes, me too. Usually Friday nights.

NAN. Actually, I think that's the only night they specify young professionals only. I mean the other nights it's for young anybody, but on Friday night it's specifically for young professionals, so that's why I come on Friday.

BOB. Yes. That's why I only come on Friday too. It's four dollars more to get in, but it's worth every cent to be with someone more in your league. You know what I mean?

NAN. I know what you mean.

BOB. Someone you have something in common with. You know what I mean?

NAN. I know what you mean. Your peers.

BOB. My what?

NAN. Your peers.

BOB. Peers?

NAN. Your equals. Someone you have something in common with.

BOB. Right. Young professionals.

NAN. Exactly!

BOB. Exactly…I always wondered how old one has to be before they can't consider themselves a young professional anymore.

NAN. I think they're very liberal about that. At the door there's a sign giving seniors ten percent off.

BOB. Really? That's good to know. Takes the pressure off.

So what is it you do, young professional Nan?

NAN. I'm a manicurist.

BOB. Oh. How nice. Must be interesting.

NAN. I could tell some stories.

BOB. *(Laughing and going along with her)* I'll bet you could.

(A beat)

I had a manicure once.

NAN. Oh, good for you.

BOB. Yes. *(Indicates)* That's how I lost the tip of my index finger. The girl doing it fell asleep.

NAN. *(Nods)* That sometimes happens.

BOB. Yes. I heard that it does.

NAN. Nowadays, nothing's without risk.

BOB. So it seems. I lost part of my ear getting a haircut.

NAN. No?

BOB. Yes.

NAN. I'm so sorry.

BOB. My circumcision was a horror story.

NAN. Really?

BOB. I was eight days old, but I remember it vividly.

NAN. There are some things you never forget.

BOB. Never. So, you're a manicurist.

NAN. Yes. And you're a painter.

BOB. *(Impressed)* Yes. Yes I am. I am a painter. How did you know?

NAN. Your nails. That's the first thing I notice on a person, their nails. You have blue and orange paint under them.

BOB. You're very perceptive. I'm impressed.

(Looks at nails)

Blue and orange. Yes, I'm painting a Howard Johnson's motel.

NAN. Oh, then you're not a picture-painter. You're basically a painter-painter.

BOB. Yes, basically a painter-painter. But a professional painter-painter of course.

NAN. Of course. Otherwise, why would you be here on Friday night when it's only for young professionals?

BOB. Exactly. So, Nan. You're here every Friday and so am I. How come I've never seen you before?

NAN. You have.

BOB. I have?

NAN. I used to be a brunette. This week I decided to become a blonde.

BOB. Really? Very nice choice. By any chance when you were a brunette, did I ever ask you to dance?

NAN. As a matter of fact, you did. Just last week.

BOB. Really? And how did we do together?

NAN. I turned you down.

BOB. Oh. I get a lot of that. I just don't understand why.

NAN. It's your jacket.

BOB. My jacket? What's wrong with my jacket?

NAN. I'm surprised you haven't noticed. It's the same pattern as the wallpaper here.

BOB. (*Looks at his jacket and then looks around at the walls*) Oh, my. So it is. Funny I didn't notice that.

NAN. I've watched when you've danced with other girls. When you got too close to the wall it looks like they're dancing with a bobbling head. It's not very attractive.

BOB. No, I guess it wouldn't be. Listen, what if I took my jacket off? Would you dance with me then?

NAN. I'm afraid not.

BOB. No? Why?

NAN. It's your shirt and pants. They're the exact color as the dance floor. I think I'd just be asking for trouble. I like your tie, though. Except for that red stain in the middle. I think it's ketchup or something.

BOB. I had pasta for dinner.

NAN. There's a little sauce on your chin too.

BOB. Oh, really.

(He lifts the tip of his tie and begins dabbing his chin with it)

Am I getting it?

NAN. A little to the left.

(Bob continues dabbing)

NAN *(CONTINUED)* There. I think you got it all.

BOB. Thanks. Well, maybe next Friday I'll wear a different jacket and a different shirt and a different tie. Maybe you'll dance with me then.

NAN. Actually, I don't think I will.

BOB. Why not? We seem to be having a nice conversation. We have a lot in common. We're both professionals.

NAN. Well, the truth is, Bob, I've been coming here for twelve years, always hopeful that one day I would meet the man of my dreams.

BOB. Not an unreasonable expectation.

NAN. I don't think so either. Anyway, you see basically I'm a very practical, level headed girl…

BOB. Which I sensed immediately.

NAN. Well, I have a feeling that once I start dancing with you, well, I might enjoy it a little too much, being held close, our bodies touching, swaying to the music, our hearts pulsating…

BOB. Sounds good. So?

NAN. So what if, moved by that kind of moment, I let you talk me into coming home with you? We'd go to bed and it would probably be wonderful and suddenly we become an item and the next thing you know we're married.

BOB. Great. And what would be wrong with that?

NAN. Can I be honest, Bob?

BOB. Of course, Nan.

NAN. You're not really the man of my dreams.

BOB. No?

NAN. Not by a long shot. Oh, I could probably make do and we would most likely get along fine, but what if during our marriage, my dream man finally shows up? I'd feel really cheated and I'm afraid that would slowly become an issue with us.

BOB. *(Nods)* I see. You're a bit of a nut case, aren't you, Nan?

NAN. I have a few problems.

BOB. Well, you don't have to worry about my trying to take you home with me. I couldn't even if I wanted to.

NAN. The circumcision?

BOB. No. Not at all. You see, I still live at home with my mother. I'm not allowed to bring women to my room.

NAN. Oh, my. That's not something a girl would put in the plus column, is it?

BOB. I guess not. But you have to look at it from my side of the fence. Not only does my mom cook for me and do my laundry, every now and then she'll go out and wash my car. A guy can't give up a deal like that so easily.

NAN. Well, Bob, we all have to make choices in this world.

BOB. Yes, I'm afraid we do. Anyway, since it seems like a hopeless situation between you and me, I'm going to move on. There's a girl down at the other end who has glasses as thick as soda pop bottles. Maybe she won't notice my jacket.

NAN. Good for you. You must never give up hope.

BOB. My feelings exactly.

(Rises)

Well, it's been nice talking to you, Nan.

NAN. And you too, Bob. See you around.

BOB. Yeah. And I really like your blonde hair, I really do.

(He EXITS. Nan takes a beat and sighs)

NAN. It's so hard these days being a single, young professional. So very, very hard.

(The LIGHTS SLOWLY FADE on her)

End of Act I, Scene 2

ACT I

Scene 3

PURGATORY

TIME: *The present. Early afternoon.*

PLACE: *A cafe.*

RICHARD *is seated at a restaurant table. He has a drink in front of him.* **JACK** *approaches him. Both men are in their early forties.*

JACK. Hello Richard.

RICHARD. Hello, Jack. It's so nice of you to agree to meet me.

JACK. *(Sitting)* Well, I really didn't want to, but you were so damn insistent and then when you told me you had some good news for me, I was sort of curious.

RICHARD. Yes, yes. Great news for you as a matter of fact. How about a drink first?

JACK. No, thanks. I have a tennis date this afternoon.

RICHARD. Yeah. Tennis. I ought to get back into it. Maybe one day soon I will. Well, let's just get right to it then. Look, I know you're still pissed off at me, not that I blame you, but well, I think that when you hear what I'm about to tell you, you'll see why I was so excited to see you and tell you this wonderful news as soon as I could. Jack, I've decided to give up your wife.

JACK. My ex-wife.

RICHARD. Yes. Of course. Your ex-wife. Anyway, you can have her back and the kids too. I won't be in the way anymore.

JACK. Is that so?

RICHARD. Look, I don't want you feeling sorry for me, but over these past two years that I've been husband to Brenda and father to little Brian and Danny, I've come to realize that I could never replace you in their hearts, not ever. I was never able to replace the great love and need they had for you.

JACK. Oh, come on. You're not trying to tell me Brenda loved me. Not after the horrible way she kicked me out to marry you. God, all my suits on the front lawn, my underwear hanging from a tree...

RICHARD. I swear, Jack, the poor woman never stopped regretting the day she divorced you. The way she cries herself to sleep at night, looking at your wedding pictures whenever she thought I wasn't around...

JACK. That's strictly from her drinking. She gets kind of maudlin when she drinks. When I was married to her, she used to take out a bottle of bourbon and a picture of George Clooney and do the same thing.

RICHARD. You know about her drinking? Then it isn't a recent thing?

JACK. Are you kidding. Brenda was in rehab six times when I was married to her.

RICHARD. I didn't know that.

JACK. Well, I didn't want to bring it up because I didn't know what good it would do.

RICHARD. What about her chronic depression and her constant yelling and screaming? Did you know about that too?

JACK. I loved Brenda, but she was wacky as a fruit cake. I was just hoping it wouldn't rub off on the kids. By the way, how are the kids? I haven't seen them since Brenda accused me of being a child abuser and a sexual predator and had the court ban me from ever having contact with them again.

RICHARD. Well, that was just legal maneuvering. I'm sure she didn't really mean anything bad by it. Anyway, outside of missing you desperately, the kids are fine.

JACK. Really? I heard from one of Brenda's cousins that little Brian was thrown out of school for bringing a gun into the class room?

RICHARD. Well, he's ten years old. He's at a very difficult stage. But Danny's doing wonderfully. Very nice boy, very quiet.

JACK. I heard he's stoned on crack all the time.

RICHARD. Well, you know high school kids today. It's hard making contact with some of them.

JACK. She also said I probably wouldn't recognize him with all the tattoos.

RICHARD. Probably not. But I'm sure it's just a passing phase. Anyway, Jack, it looks like you won in the end and so I'm going to do the honorable thing and bow out. I give them all back to you, Jack. Your wife, your kids, your house, your dogs…Now, I've worked it out so that I can go to Vegas, get a quickie divorce and you can jump right back in and pick up where you left off, remarry the girl of your dreams, get the kids back and return to being the happy family that you once were. And I'll tell you what. When you remarry Brenda, I insist on throwing you both a wedding. What do you say?

JACK. Really, gee, I don't know. I'm not sure I want to do that.

RICHARD. What do you mean, you're not sure? What kind of talk is that. That doesn't sound like a loving husband and father to me.

JACK. I know, but I don't have to be that anymore. You are. And frankly, between you and me, I prefer leaving it that way. I'll level with you, Richard. When Brenda told me she was leaving me for you, I wasn't very happy about it. And I wasn't too happy when she got complete custody of the kids and I wasn't too happy when the courts allowed you to adopt them. But you know, the longer I was away from that situation, the better I started to feel. Richard, old pal, I would rather eat a live octopus than jump back into that madhouse.

RICHARD. Please, you can't think that way. Once you get

back in the picture, I assure you, everything will change back to normal.

JACK. Normal? Come on. Don't be an idiot. My life with my family was never normal. We gave the word "dysfunctional" a bad name. No, Richard, I'm leaving things the way they are. I'm off the hook and I'm staying off the hook. Well, I need to be going...

(He starts to rise. Richard pulls him back down)

RICHARD. Look, Jack, I'm not going to bullshit you anymore. It was all a big mistake. Your family is ruining me. Your kids are driving me crazy and so is your wife. The therapy bills are costing me a fortune. The truth is, I can't afford a divorce because with the alimony I'd have to pay Brenda and the child support I'd now be obligated to pay, I'd have nothing left. My life has been hell since I married your wife. Your kids hate my guts. Little Brian tied me to a chair and tried to set me on fire four times. It isn't fair and I can't take it anymore. I want out, do you hear me. I want out.

JACK. It seems God works in mysterious ways, doesn't he? Well, I need to get to my tennis game. Then afterwards, there's a singles cocktail party where there are three chicks to every guy. It's a wonderful world out there, Richard, and I've never been happier in my life. Give Brenda and the kids my best.

(Jack rises)

Oh, by the way, if I never told you this before, thanks for everything. See you.

(Goes off. Richard drops his head to the table. The LIGHTS DIM TO BLACK)

End of Act I, Scene 3

ACT I

Scene 4

MAY I RECOMMEND THE CROW?

TIME: *The present. Early evening.*

PLACE: *An elegant restaurant.*

JOYCE, *a woman in her late forties, is at a restaurant table studying the menu.* **CHARLES**, *the waiter, also in his late forties, approaches. He is in a tuxedo.*

CHARLES. Good evening. My name is Charles, I'll be your waiter tonight. Would madam care for anything to drink before she orders?

JOYCE. No, thank you. Not right now. Maybe with my dinner…

(As she looks up)

I'll have a…Charles? Oh, my God, Charles, it's you.

CHARLES. *(Coldly)* Yes, Joyce. It's me. Or what's left of me, after you and your two bit lawyers took me to the cleaners. May I go over tonight's specials?

JOYCE. Yes, yes of course. It's obvious you haven't forgiven me, have you, Charles?

CHARLES. Forgiven you? For what? For leaving me without a nickel to my name. Destitute, penniless. A broken man. This evening our featured soup is a delicate creamed asparagus, sprinkled ever so lightly with bits of black forest ham, elevated with a dab of cilantro oil amidst a thin cushion of freshly chopped basil.

JOYCE. Sounds exquisite. Okay, I'll start with that. Look, Charles, isn't it about time to let bygones be bygones?

Our divorce is all behind us now. Let's try to be good sports about it and go on with our lives.

CHARLES. It's apparent you can. Why not? You got the apartment, the business, the savings account, everything. Would you care for a small house salad after your soup? It's a very enticing presentation of heirloom tomatoes, butter lettuce, shaved fennel and wafer thin baby carrots tossed ever so delicately in a prickly pear vinaigrette.

JOYCE. Oh, yes. That might be nice. I'll have that also. Anyway, Charles, you only have yourself to blame for what happened to you. You wouldn't have lost everything if you didn't try to hide your assets from me in another state.

CHARLES. I wasn't hiding the money from you, Joyce, I was hiding it from the government. I was planning to be more than fair with you but no, you had to be a pig about it and threaten to tell the authorities if I didn't hand it all over to you. Now, for our four star entree, tonight we are very proud to offer a succulently grilled sesame coated veal chop, atop a bevy of sauteed wild mushrooms, surrounded by a plush sea of pureed broccoli and Peruvian potatoes.

JOYCE. Oh, that sounds interesting. Let me keep that in mind. Anyway, so help me, Charles, after paying all the investigators and auditors I had to hire, I only wound up with three or four hundred thousand dollars at the most. Still it was nothing compared to all the money I discovered you spent on that little tramp you left me for. Be grateful you were able to make a deal with me. If the IRS ever found out about that hidden stash, tonight you'd be waiting on tables in Sing Sing. You know, I'm not really in the mood for veal.

CHARLES. No, veal. Very well, perhaps then may I suggest our fabulous Chicken San Carlos. Carlos being our chef, he takes extra pains with this one. It's a skinless breast of chicken marinated in a bourbon brown sugar peppercorn sauce, garlic pan fried to a lovely golden hue and ringed by a glorious avalanche of braised cucumbers and roasted coconut risotto. Bitch that you are, Joyce, you couldn't be satisfied with just my money, you had to go for the jugular vein. God, that judge was such a bastard. Why he awarded you control of the business is beyond me.

JOYCE. Trust me, Charles, no one was more surprised than me when Harry handed down that decision. Even I thought it was a little harsh.

CHARLES. Harry? You called that crook of a judge, Harry? Damn, I thought there was something fishy going on between you two. The way he kept winking at you all through the trial. He should be disbarred, that son-of-a-bitch.

JOYCE. You know, I believe I'll pass on the chicken too. No matter how it's disguised, I always find chicken to end up just being chicken. What do you have tonight that's really adventurous?

CHARLES. Adventurous? Dear woman, you are in luck because tonight we have an unbelievable mixed grill consisting of quail, ostrich and venison basted in a cinnamon huckleberry merlot sauce, shamelessly smothered with a riotous melee of balsamic fig and avocado slices. How does that sound?

JOYCE. Intriguing. Extremely intriguing. Anyway, you'll be happy to know that Harry's not a judge anymore. Since I was awarded the company, I hired him to run things. Fortunately with Harry's connections, he's taken the business public and it's quadrupled in value. It's too bad you had to sell your share to pay the divorce lawyers. You could have become a very rich man. I saw on the menu you had seafood paella.

CHARLES. Yes. Forgive me. I should have recommended that earlier. Scallops, shrimp and clams slowly cooked in a succulent tarragon broth. I hear it's wonderful. I've never tried it because I can't afford to eat in this restaurant. That goddamn lawyer of mine! I couldn't have gotten a worse one. I kept telling him I was being screwed, but all he did was tell me to just sit back and trust him. I did and look where it's gotten me.

JOYCE. Yes, you did seem to be let down by Wendell. But I talked to him afterwards and he told me he just wasn't on his toes for that one. You know, when I came in, I saw someone eating a lobster that looked fabulous.

CHARLES. Wendell? You were friendly with my lawyer too? Shit! We do have lobster, but between you and me it's very overpriced.

JOYCE. Yes, actually Wendell and I have become very close. As a matter of fact, he's on my board of directors now that he's stopped practicing law. You know, I think I'll have the lobster. What's money for anyway? It looked like it was served in some sort of sauce.

CHARLES. Yes, a garlic butter that's out of this world. Sometimes when a customer leaves a little left over, I dip some bread in it and it serves as my dinner. So basically, what you're telling me Joyce is that I was railroaded and screwed by your lawyer, by my lawyer and the judge.

JOYCE. Basically, yes, Charles. But you shouldn't feel that bad. After all, you did get to appeal the case to a higher court. Maybe I will order a glass of wine now.

CHARLES. Very good. With the lobster may I suggest a white Zinfandel.

JOYCE. Perfect.

CHARLES. Yeah, some higher court. It was my rotten luck that I got the toughest female judge in the county. She ruled against me on every single issue. I don't know what her goddamn problem was.

JOYCE. You don't? Well, I'll tell you. That tramp of yours who you left me for, was the judge's ex-girlfriend.

CHARLES. Oh, no. My sweet little Laverne was a lesbian? I had no idea.

JOYCE. Yes, the detectives I hired to investigate you two were extraordinary. They left no stone unturned. I'm afraid, Charles, there was no way anything was ever going to work out for you. By the way, you'll be happy to know the judge and your sweet little Laverne are back together again and they're buying a ranch in Oregon.

CHARLES. How do you know that?

JOYCE. I'm loaning them the money for the down payment.

CHARLES. Look, I can't go on. This has been much too painful for me. I'm sorry but I'm going to have another waiter take over.

JOYCE. Are you sure you want to do that, Charles? You know, I tip twenty-five percent.

CHARLES. You do? Twenty-five? That's quite a bit. Damn it, I really could use the money. I've got my eye on a new pair of shoes. You can't believe how many I wear out on this job. Okay, okay. I'll stay. I'll go put in your order.

JOYCE. Thank you. And Charles, I'm not telling you this just to make you feel good, but you're really an excellent waiter and so help me, every time I come here, I'll be sure to ask for your section. That should put you in very solid with your boss.

CHARLES. That's very kind, Joyce. I'm genuinely touched.

JOYCE. Good. Oh, one more thing.

CHARLES. Yes, Joyce.

JOYCE. I'll be sure to leave a little of the lobster garlic butter sauce for you to dip some bread in.

(FADE OUT)

End of Act I

ACT II

Scene 1

CLEARING THE AIR

TIME: The present.
PLACE: A bare stage.

CLARK *and* **JILL**, *a couple in their late twenties, early thirties, are going at it, face to face. Their anger builds.*

JILL. You bastard!

CLARK. You bitch!

JILL. You bastard!

CLARK. You bitch!

JILL. You bastard!

CLARK. You bitch!

JILL. You bastard!

CLARK. You bitch!

JILL. You bastard!

CLARK. You bitch!

(They both take a deep breath and then relax)

CLARK *(CONTINUED)* How was it for you?

JILL. Great. And you?

CLARK. Never better. Well, off to work.

JILL. Love ya.

CLARK. Love ya right back.

(They kiss quickly on the lips. Clark EXITS. LIGHTS UP on **EMMA**, *a contemporary, who has witnessed this. She crosses to Jill)*

EMMA. And you and Clark do this every morning?

JILL. Every morning.

EMMA. Weekends too?

JILL. Yes. Although on weekends we usually do it at night when we almost mean it. That's really intense. Of course, you have to realize that's when we're together the most.

EMMA. And it works? It really works?

JILL. Fabulously! You see when you say these things to one another and you don't really mean it, then when you say these things to one another and you do mean it, the whole edge is gone.

EMMA. And you started this on your honeymoon?

JILL. The third day when it looked like the marriage was in the toilet. We've been together over five years and since we've been doing this, we have never had one major confrontation.

EMMA. That's unbelievable.

JILL. The fact that we're still together is a miracle. People who knew us didn't give the marriage a year. Maybe that's why we got such awful gifts. We actually got a set of those cheap Ginzu steak knives you see on TV. Can you imagine that?

EMMA. Well, there was a certain loss of confidence when you each had to be walked down the aisle by your therapists. Anyway, let me see if I have this straight. You bitch! You bastard! You bitch! You bastard! You bitch! You bastard! That's basically it, huh?

JILL. It just puts any brewing hostility to rest immediately. Of course you're not limited to just those words. Those were the words that seemed to fit our needs the best. We fiddled around with others, you know like "asshole" and "shit for brains", but they seemed to be a little too endearing. It actually worked against us.

EMMA. Well, bitch and bastard seems like it could fill the bill for us.

JILL. I honestly believe that without this little routine in our life, Clark and I would just be another typical, pathetic, miserable, upwardly mobile American couple paying off two BMW's, four maxed out credit cards, a mortgage that could choke a horse and blaming each other for being in this mess.

EMMA. There's so much of that going around, isn't there? Well, I'm very excited about this and I'm going to run it by Harrison tonight.

JILL. Good for you. I'm off to yoga.

EMMA. Have fun. And thanks again.

(LIGHTS OUT on Jill and UP on **HARRISON**, *also in his late twenties, early thirties, as* **EMMA** *crosses to him)*

HARRISON. Let me get this straight. You want us to swear at one another?

EMMA. Every morning and at night on weekends. And try not to think of it as swearing. Try thinking of it as clearing the air. Jill and Clark haven't had one major confrontation since they started doing this.

HARRISON. They're not my favorite couple, you know. They still haven't sent us a thank you note for those Ginzu steak knives we sent them. Besides, I think our marriage is just fine. We don't need to resort to name calling and using hurtful words. That's not the way we operate honey, and I really don't think we should start now.

EMMA. You mean you don't hold any resentments, about me or about our life together?

HARRISON. Well, of course I do. All married people do. But it's not like they're major. I mean, sure, I get annoyed now and then about your going to lunch with your old boyfriends and not coming home for a few days. Yeah, that bothers me. But I'm sure you've experienced some little irritations I've caused you.

EMMA. You mean like when we're out for a drive and I criticize your speeding and you stop the car, drag me out by my hair and make me walk home?

HARRISON. Yeah. And I'm not very fond of all the times that you do get home, you call up your brother and have him come over and beat the crap out of me. That gets a little bit irritating.

EMMA. I hate how mad you get every time I discuss your drinking. How it always ends up with you coming at me with a baseball bat.

HARRISON. Well, if you noticed I don't do that anymore since you bought a gun and shot me in the leg.

EMMA. So you see, we do have issues Harrison. And as trivial as they might seem, I really feel that if we don't nip them in the bud, it's very possible they're just going to fester into something bigger. The last thing I want Harrison, is for this marriage of ours to come apart. Do you remember how awful it was being in the singles market?

HARRISON. I know. You really meet some weirdos out there.

EMMA. That's why we've got to do everything we can to protect what we have. You can be honest with me. Haven't you ever wanted to call me a bitch?

HARRISON. Well, sure. Just about every day that we've been together. But name calling is so petty and I just hate thinking of us as petty people.

EMMA. Sometimes a change of direction can be very refreshing.

HARRISON. Look, I'll tell you what. We're having dinner with the Freemonts tonight. I know some time during the evening you'll say something stupid to piss me off and then we'll come home and start throwing dishes and pots at each other. Then the neighbors will call the police and I'll have to spend a couple of days in jail again. Maybe a wiser time to start this name calling would be right after we got home.

EMMA. That's why I love you, Harrison. Your a sick bastard, but you're definitely the voice of reason. Hey, did you hear what I just called you? A sick bastard. And even though I didn't mean to, it felt great.

HARRISON. Really? Well, I'm happy for you bitch but… Hey! Hey listen to me now. I called you bitch and I didn't mean it either. And you're right, it felt very good. Very freeing.

EMMA. Yes, you did, you bastard, you did. Bastard!

HARRISON. Bitch!

EMMA. Bastard!

HARRISON. Bitch! Wow, I like this. What do you say we cancel the Freemonts and have a real go at it, huh bitch?

EMMA. I'd love to, you bastard.

HARRISON. Then let's do it, you bitch!

EMMA. You bastard!

HARRISON. You bitch!

EMMA. Bastard!

HARRISON. Bitch! I despise you and everything about you. Every morning I wake up and wish you were dead.

EMMA. You do?

HARRISON. How I hate you. Your phony smile, your stupid laugh, your slimy touch, your scaly feet, the three little hairs that grow on your chest.

EMMA. Uh, Harrison, I think you may be straying a little from the original concept.

HARRISON. Every night I dream about you rotting away in a shallow grave that I personally dug for you, you bitch. Your face being eaten away by worms.

EMMA. Excuse me, Harrison, I suspect you might be crossing over the line a bit.

HARRISON. You little slut bitch. I would rather sleep with a disease infested banshee than you.

EMMA. Harrison…

HARRISON. Every day spent with you is a nightmare, bitch. Every minute is a living hell.

EMMA. Uh, Harrison…

(During the following Emma goes to her purses and pulls out a revolver)

HARRISON. What I'd give to just hold your head under water, watching your face squirm in horror, gasping for your final breath, your eyes bulging from their sockets as you, once and for all, realize the rage I hold in my heart for you, you lying, detestable two faced weasel pile of...

(Emma points the gun at Harrison)

EMMA. Okay, that's enough! Hold it right there.

HARRISON. Why, bitch? I'm just getting into it.

EMMA. I'm sorry, Harrison. It was a noble try, but it's simply not going to work for us. We are strictly a physically demonstrative couple and we need to remain that way. Words bring us a little too close to the truth and I don't believe our twisted but loving relationship can handle it.

(Putting gun back in her purse)

I think we'll go to the Freemonts tonight after all.

(LIGHTS START TO FADE OUT)

HARRISON. *(Softly)* Bitch! Bitch, bitch, bitch!

(Emma sighs. She knows she's opened a Pandora's box. Life can never be the same)

HARRISON *(CONTINUED)* Bitch, bitch, bitch, bitch, bitch.

EMMA. *(Another sigh. Softly)* Bastard.

(LIGHTS DIM TO BLACK)

End of Act II, Scene 1

ACT II

Scene 2

BINGO-BANGO

TIME: *The present. A Sunday afternoon.*

PLACE: *A museum*

FRED *and* **ROSALIND**, *two strangers, both in their mid-thirties, are sitting on a backless bench facing the audience. Rosalind stares ahead in awe and appreciation at an imaginary painting. Fred is sitting, waiting, not at all interested in what Rosalind is looking at. After a few moments, Rosalind speaks.*

ROSALIND. It's beautiful, isn't it?

FRED. What?

ROSALIND. The painting.

FRED. *(Not looking up)* Oh, yeah. It's okay.

ROSALIND. You're not even looking at it.

FRED. Yeah. Well, actually I'm just more or less sitting.

ROSALIND. Well, look at it.

FRED. Really, I'm not at all…

ROSALIND. *(A bit insistent)* Please. Look at it. Just look at it.

FRED. *(Looks at what Rosalind has been looking at)* Okay, I'm looking at it. Now what?

ROSALIND. Well, isn't it amazing?

FRED. *(Not getting what the big deal is)* It's a bowl of fruit.

ROSALIND. I could look at it forever.

FRED. You could? Why?

ROSALIND. Because it speaks to me. Because it is saying something extraordinary.

FRED. *(Nods. A beat as he looks at the imaginary painting again)* It's a bowl of fruit.

ROSALIND. I see much more.

FRED. I just see fruit. Two apples. An orange. A banana. Some grapes. A brown thing. It could be a rotten peach.

ROSALIND. It's a bosc pear.

FRED. Whatever. Anyway, I just see fruit.

ROSALIND. How sad. How very, very sad.

FRED. Really?

ROSALIND. Absolutely. You're missing the big picture. You're missing the pain inside a great artist. His cry for understanding, compassion and finally forgiveness.

FRED. *(A beat)* Uh huh. Frankly I never cared much for fruit, especially cantaloupe. My mother always served it for dessert. She never had pie, she never had cake. She only had cantaloupe. In a way, I'm glad she's dead.

ROSALIND. See. Already this painting is making you think. It's the colors. They tell the whole story. The reds...

FRED. The apple.

ROSALIND. Deception. The yellows.

FRED. The banana.

ROSALIND. Heartbreak. The greens and the purple. Anger and sadness. It's such a pity you don't get it. My ex-boyfriend, Herb, didn't get it either.

FRED. He just saw fruit?

ROSALIND. He wouldn't even come to the museum. He'd just stay at home in front of the TV with his beer and his chips and watch football. And after football season was basketball and then hockey and then baseball and then it started all over again. It was obvious the romance was going no where. Are you into that? All those stupid sports. One after another?

FRED. No, not at all. I hate sports.

ROSALIND. Good for you.

FRED. Porn is my big thing.

ROSALIND. Porn? Did you say porn?

FRED. I have a great collection. Over three hundred films and two thousand magazines.

ROSALIND. Porn.

FRED. Porn, smut, filth, dirt…Everybody calls it something different. But that's my weakness. Hard core shmutz. Guys with girls, guys with guys, girls with girls, whips, chains, handcuffs, batteries…you name it.

ROSALIND. *(A beat)* I understand in some circles much of that is now considered art.

FRED. Not what I've got. My stuff is strictly off with the clothes, on with the action. Bingo-bango. Bango-bingo. I love it. Maybe you ought to stop and pick up a couple of flicks for Herb. It might bring him back to life.

ROSALIND. I told you, Herb is out of my life forever. Besides relationships have to be built on more than sex. Especially for me. I happen to be a very spiritual person. I don't want just a lover. I want a true soul mate. Someone who can feel what I feel. Sense what I sense. Someone profound, with depth. And what I've found in life's journey is that you either have these gifts or you don't. That's the reason why some people like you, can look at this simple painting hanging on the wall and only see fruit, and other people like me, with my spiritual sensibilities can look at it and experience the ever eternal struggle of civilization

FRED. *(A beat after taking this all in)* Herb's a very lucky guy. Look, I'm gonna level with you. I don't give a damn about art, and I give less of a damn about this spirituality business. You want to know the only reason why I come to the museum? To pick up girls.

ROSALIND. Oh?

FRED. Yeah. I come here every Sunday strictly for that purpose. You see, this is how it works. When I see a chick sitting alone…

ROSALIND. Like I was?

FRED. Yeah. I approach her and sit down next to her…

ROSALIND. As you did with me.

FRED. Sort of. Now after a moment or so of the two of us sitting near one another, if she's interested in me, she'll casually start discussing the meaning and the merits of the particular painting she's looking at...

ROSALIND. As I did with you.

FRED. Right. And if I was interested in her, I would simply agree with everything she said, repeat most of it back to her and before you know it we'd be at my place watching a few films and bingo-bango...

ROSALIND. Bango-Bingo.

FRED. You got it.

ROSALIND. I see. And since you haven't taken that approach with me, what you're saying is...

FRED. No way, Jose. Nothing personal.

ROSALIND. Of course.

FRED. Not that you're unattractive and I wouldn't like to bingo-bango with you, but you see, I've got this little warning buzzer in my head that every now and then says red flag, red flag!

ROSALIND. And it went off with me.

FRED. I never heard it so loud. Actually, I just sat down next to you because I was tired. I've been walking through this museum for over two hours and for the first Sunday since I've been coming here there was not a single woman sitting alone.

ROSALIND. Except for me.

FRED. Except for you.

ROSALIND. And you're not interested in me.

FRED. Trust me, if I was I would have discussed fruit with you till the cows came home.

ROSALIND. Uh huh. Well, I'm sorry your day didn't work out the way you would have liked it to.

FRED. No problem. I'll just go home, put on a couple of my tapes and have sex by myself.

ROSALIND. Interesting visual.

FRED. It's not so bad. On the plus side you don't have to make small talk afterwards.

ROSALIND. This has been a very enlightening Sunday for me.

FRED. I'm glad. I always say, no one's ever too old to learn.

(**ZOE**, *a contemporary, approaches. She is totally transfixed by the painting. Unaware of anyone else's presence, she squeezes between Rosalind and Fred who make room for her as she experiences rapturous awe*)

ZOE. It's amazing, isn't it?

FRED. *(Looking her up and down)* Very.

ZOE. The pain, the torment…

FRED. Yes. Yes, pain, torment. I see those things.

ZOE. *(She turns to Fred)* The artist's cry for understanding and love.

FRED. Yeah. Yeah. And don't forget compassion and forgiveness.

ZOE. The colors. The reds.

FRED. Deception.

ZOE. The yellows.

FRED. Heartbreak.

ZOE. The greens and the purples.

FRED. Anger and sadness. Would you like to come to my place and see a few art films?

ZOE. I'd love to.

FRED. We're on our way.

(*He offers his arm to Zoe and they EXIT. Rosalind looks after them for a beat*)

ROSALIND. Well, that was a crock of shit, wasn't it?

(**IAN**, *a man also in his mid-thirties, approaches and sits down next to Rosalind. He stares at the painting as Rosalind looks him over*)

ROSALIND. *(CONTINUED)* It's really special, isn't it?

IAN. The painting?

(*He turns and looks at her for a beat*)

Yes. Very special.

ROSALIND. It's all there. Love, hate..

IAN. Apples, oranges...

ROSALIND. Reds, yellows... .

IAN. Anger and deception.

ROSALIND. Do you have any porn tapes?

IAN. Tons. Some of them are considered art.

(Rosalind rises and pulls Ian to his feet)

ROSALIND. Good. We'll watch those last.

(They EXIT)

(BLACKOUT)

End of Act II, Scene 2

ACT II

Scene 3

DINNER WITH FRIENDLY NEIGHBORS

TIME: The present. Early evening.

PLACE: A restauraunt.

DONNA *and* **NICK PALMER,** *a couple in their early thirties and* **IRENE** *and* **WAYNE OGDEN,** *a couple in their early fifties, are in a restaurant semi-circular booth studying menus. Donna puts her menu down.*

DONNA. It's really so nice of you guys to invite us out to dinner.

NICK. It really is. It was totally unexpected, but totally appreciated.

IRENE. Well, from the moment you two came over to introduce yourselves to us the other day, Wayne said to me, those are two people we should really get to know. They're so friendly, so out going...so neighborly.

WAYNE. And then to bring us a cake and a box of candy. That's what we should have brought you.

NICK. Well, it's just our way of saying hello.

WAYNE. Well, it was really...well, very...

DONNA. Friendly.

IRENE. Yes. Very friendly.

DONNA. Well, isn't that the way neighbors are supposed to be?

WAYNE. Absolutely. Irene and I thrive on friendly neighbors.

NICK. Because it's obvious you're friendly people.

DONNA. In our old neighborhood, everyone was extremely friendly. We were practically family, that's how close we all were.

NICK. We'd do everything together. Go on camping trips, picnics, babysit for each other. People would go in and out of each other's house like it was their own.

IRENE. Sounds quite warm and fuzzy.

DONNA. Oh, it was. And it was so sad we had to leave. But Nick got this fantastic job opportunity and we couldn't turn it down.

NICK. But I told her. Donna, I said, people are not that different. I know we will find the same kind of wonderful friendly community where ever we go because if we're wonderful and friendly neighbors then our neighbors will be wonderful and friendly. That's just how it works. And friendly is family.

WAYNE. Friendly and family. They're my two favorite F words.

DONNA. We know it's going to be another marvelous community experience.

WAYNE. Well, look, I don't want you two to be too disappointed, but while some people in our area might be the nice cozy type...

IRENE. Like us.

WAYNE. Yes, like us. There are others that, well, let's say they could be very disappointing.

NICK. I have a feeling you're trying to warn us about someone.

IRENE. Well, Wayne is a little down on the Conrads right now.

DONNA. Aren't they the people next door to you? They seemed very nice when we went over and introduced ourselves to them.

WAYNE. Yes, they do give that impression.

IRENE. Now there's a case where I felt they were family more than friends.

WAYNE. *(Sadly)* Yes. Yes, that's exactly what I thought.

NICK. It sounds like they somehow let you down.

WAYNE. Let us down big time. Let me be blunt. What kind of people call themselves friends and then won't co-sign on a hundred thousand dollar loan for you?

(Nick and Donna look at each other in surprised amazement)

IRENE. Wayne was so hurt when they turned him down. I just saw the poor man's heart break in half. Think of it. We knew these people for over eight months. Wayne was over at their house all the time. In fact, he practically lived there.

WAYNE. They always had great booze. I'd fix myself a double scotch on the rocks and I'd sit in their living room for hours. Irene would have to drag me out of that house almost every night.

IRENE. Well, carrying him out, might be a better description. Wayne has a little drinking problem.

NICK. Oh, sorry to hear that.

WAYNE. It's not a problem. It's more of a bad habit. But then so is too much coffee, right?

(Nick and Donna are starting to get a little uncomfortable)

NICK. Yeah, I guess so.

IRENE. Well, fortunately they're not the only ones who we can go to for help. There's also our good friends the Paulsen's across the street.

DONNA. Yes. We met them too. They seemed very nice also.

WAYNE. Yeah, good old Tommy Paulsen. I'm more than sure I'll be able to get him to co-sign the loan for me. We're very close. I always borrow his car every time mine gets repossessed.

IRENE. I just hope Beverly is not still angry with you for throwing up on her new carpets.

WAYNE. Even so, I'd really be surprised if old Tommy weaseled out of co-signing. Of course if he does, we've got these great new neighbors now.

(Reaches across table and pats him on the hand.)

Right, Nick old pal.

NICK. Us? You'd want us to co-sign a hundred thousand dollar loan?

WAYNE. No big deal. I can have you in and out of the bank in ten minutes.

NICK. Well, uh, I'm not sure co-signing would be the right thing for us. I mean we just took out a big loan for our place. I'm not sure the bank would...

WAYNE. Approve of you? Forget it. I already checked. You two have great credit. Besides, the people at the bank aren't that bright.

IRENE. Wayne is so right. You can't believe what we got away with, with our last loan.

DONNA. You had another loan?

WAYNE. We still have it. That's why we need this new loan. They keep threatening to foreclose on our house. Anyway, you have nothing to worry about. Just in case things get a little sticky, I'll work it out so that you can put a lien on my business. You'll be out of the woods in no time at all.

NICK. Really. Just what is your business?

IRENE. Wayne is the biggest goldfish distributor in Southern California.

DONNA. Goldfish?

WAYNE. Take it from me, it doesn't sound like much, but like it says on all on my business cards, "there's gold in goldfish."

IRENE. Isn't that cute? Wayne made that up himself.

NICK. So why don't you just put your business up as collateral and then you won't need anyone to co-sign.

WAYNE. Unfortunately, it's not that easy. Because of the poor economy, the drop in employment, well, the carnival business has been very slow.

DONNA. The carnival business?

IRENE. Yes. That's who Wayne sells most of his gold fish to. Carnivals. Toss a ping pong ball in a dish and try to win a fish. It's so much fun. Maybe after dinner we can come back to our house and play it. We've got the dishes and the goldfish.

NICK. Just as a curiosity, Wayne, how much do you charge for a gold fish?

WAYNE. Well, wholesale, about a quarter a fish. Let me tell you, when business is good, it's great. Sometimes I sell two hundred goldfish a day.

DONNA. Really? Gee, at twenty-five cents a fish that only comes to fifty dollars.

WAYNE. Is that all? Well, I don't get into that. I let my accountant crunch the numbers. I just sell the fish. So what do you guys say? Can I count on you to co-sign for me? That way I don't have to bother the Paulsen's, who between you and me, I have bad feelings about getting involved with.

DONNA. *(She has no idea what to say)* Nick?

NICK. Well…Well, just what would this loan be for? I mean are you planning to expand your business?

WAYNE. Expand it? How?

NICK. Well, maybe take in another line, like exotic fish… or maybe parakeets.

WAYNE. No. I'm strictly a goldfish guy. The one thing I don't want to do is spread myself too thin. I've seen too many guys go under doing that.

DONNA. So the loan would be for…?

WAYNE. Just every day expenses.

IRENE. You know, groceries, the cleaners…vacations

WAYNE. For sure one of those super size wide screen TV's.

IRENE. For years Wayne's been talking about getting a second home in the country some where.

WAYNE. Yeah. I desperately need a place where I can just unwind, get away from the pressures of everyday life.

IRENE. And no one deserves it more than you, dear. And the first people we'll have over are these two nice folks.

WAYNE. That's a given. You know, life is really a hoot. A few days ago I thought we were really in the toilet. Then fate sent us you two and now look how everything's turned around. Just goes to show you. It's never over till it's over.

(Wayne picks up his menu)

Now what do you say we order? For some reason I seemed to have worked up an appetite.

(Looks at the menu)

God, look at the prices here. Thirty six bucks for a steak.

DONNA. The chicken isn't bad. It's only sixteen ninety-five. I'll have that.

NICK. Me too. Chicken is going to be fine.

WAYNE. Ahh, the hell with it. Steak is what I want, steak is what I'll get.

IRENE. I'll have the same.

WAYNE. By the way, Nick, can you put this on your card? Mine are all maxed out. I'll get dinner next time.

IRENE. I hear the desserts are great here.

WAYNE. Anyway, you two, it's great to have you guys in the neighborhood and I'll be over with the loan papers first thing in the morning.

NICK. No. No you won't.

(He rises and motions for Donna to get up)

You won't be over to our house ever, because we're not inviting you and never will. I wouldn't co-sign for a bag of kitty litter for you people. Think of us as just one more neighbor that wants nothing to do with you, like the Conrads and the Paulsen's and...and I'm sure who ever else lives on the block. I'm sorry we ever tried to be friends with you. You're...you're nuts. Come on, Donna. We're going home. I'll buy you a fish sandwich at MacDonald's.

(Nick and Donna EXIT. Wayne takes a beat and sighs.)

WAYNE. Well, there's another friendly neighbor we'll never have to worry about bugging us.

IRENE. Maybe the problem is our house looks too inviting. What if we put a chain link fence around it and got a pit bull for the front yard?

WAYNE. Not a bad idea. I like that. Anyway, let's order. I'm starved. I think I'll have the chicken.

IRENE. Good idea. I'll have that too.

(BLACKOUT)

End of Act I, Scene 3

ACT II

Scene 4

HOLLYWOOD LOVE STORY

LIGHTS UP on ALAN *and* KAREN, *a couple in their mid-thirties. They sit together on a small backless bench facing the audience.*

ALAN. *(Not looking directly at Karen)* What a night. What a lousy, awful, night.

(Karen says nothing, trying to ignore him)

What a stupid, miserable, boring, dreadful night.

(Karen continues to ignore him. He then turns to her to make sure she'll be aware of him)

What a crappy, stinky, shitty, pissy, pukey, night.

KAREN. *(Takes a beat and nods)* I had a nice time.

ALAN. You did?

KAREN. Yes, I did.

ALAN. You're just saying that to annoy me.

KAREN. You made up your mind not to have a nice time even before we left the house.

ALAN. How can you say that?

KAREN. Because it's true. I know you, Alan. When you make up your mind not to enjoy something, you don't and you made up your mind not to enjoy David and Trish's party.

ALAN. How can you enjoy hor d'oeuvres that you can't identify, chicken that was cooked to death and wine that was obviously run through a horse's penis.

KAREN. You didn't seem to have any trouble drinking the wine.

ALAN. I had to do something to kill the taste of the chicken.

KAREN. For your information, Alan, it wasn't chicken they served. It was squab.

ALAN. Squab? That's even worse. Squab's a pigeon. They're all over the goddamn planet shitting on cars. Damn. I ate a pigeon. Now I really hate this evening.

KAREN. Well, I thought it was a nice party. In fact, I enjoyed it more than the one we gave.

ALAN. How can you even compare the two. At least at our party we served red meat.

KAREN. We served chili and three people got sick.

ALAN. Well, since one of them was my agent and the other two were my lawyer and his wife, I don't feel that bad. I don't know why we let that stupid caterer talk us into that rodeo theme. I'm glad everyone's suing him. Anyway, thank goodness the night's over. It set a bench mark for boredom.

KAREN. Sometimes I wonder, Alan. Could I have found a more negative man to marry?

ALAN. I am not negative. I am discriminating. The fact that I don't like ninety-nine percent of the things in this world only shows that I have taste.

KAREN. I would be thrilled if you could point out the one percent of the things in this world you do like. I doubt very much whether you'd even find your name on that list.

ALAN. Are you insinuating that I don't like myself?

KAREN. Yes. If you did, you wouldn't torture yourself as much as you do.

ALAN. I'm a screenwriter. I need to be tortured. And some people who have read my stuff think I deserve to be tortured.

KAREN. You know that's not true. You're very successful and very respected. You've got to lay off yourself.

ALAN. At one time you loved my self-deprecating humor.

KAREN. Yes. At one time I thought it showed humility. It seemed clever and gracious. Now after three years of marriage I realize it's just whining. You actually don't want to be happy, do you?

ALAN. Happiness does not make sense. At least an unhappy person has a goal. He strives to be happy. Then what is the goal of the happy person? He hasn't any. He's screwed. Besides, being unhappy makes people think you have depth. A good grim look on your face makes them think you're really concerned about world events. I actually think unhappiness has gotten me more work than I deserve.

KAREN. I was hoping I could make you happy, Alan.

ALAN. Really? Why would you give yourself such an impossible task?

KAREN. Because I love you.

ALAN. Maybe you need to find a more deserving charity.

(They look at each other. Karen sighs hopelessly. The LIGHTS GO OUT on them. LIGHTS UP on DAVID and TRISH. David is in his late-forties. Trish is in her early-thirties. They also sit on a small, backless bench facing the audience)

DAVID. *(Enthused)* Great party. I thought it went very well.

TRISH. *(Not as enthused)* Yes, it was very nice.

DAVID. I think as parties go, it was one of our better ones.

TRISH. Maybe.

DAVID. You don't think so?

TRISH. I think it was very nice. All the parties we throw are very nice.

DAVID. Everyone seemed to enjoy themselves. Most people stayed until after eleven. That's very rare for a party made up of mostly married people. As usual, the only one not enjoying himself was Alan.

TRISH. How do you know?

DAVID. He kept looking at his watch all evening. The man

enjoys nothing. They should make Karen a saint. How such a sweet, caring woman puts up with him is beyond me.

TRISH. Maybe you should stop inviting him.

DAVID. He's a very gifted writer. It's very important for a producer to be seen with creative people no matter how uncomfortable they make you feel. Anyway, he wasn't the only one with a long face.

TRISH. Oh.

DAVID. I noticed you had one too. In fact, every time you stood next to Alan you looked like a pair of book ends.

TRISH. I'm sorry. It's just that I seem to have such a hard time at these things. I've never been good at superficial sincerity. All the phony hugging and kissing and concern everyone shows each other when you know that as soon as they all get in their cars they're going to have a million terrible things to say about everyone.

DAVID. Honey, this is Hollywood. Gossip and slander is one of the perks. Look, Trish, you know as well as I do, this business operates on being social. As uncomfortable as it is for you, I need to do this.

TRISH. It's just gotten so difficult for me, David.

DAVID. It never used to be. Maybe one day we should get into it a little deeper, unless you need to talk about it tonight. Do you?

TRISH. *(Sighs)* I don't know. I don't know.

DAVID. *(Looks at her for a beat)* We're in trouble, Trish, aren't we?

TRISH. Yes, David. We're in trouble.

(David looks at her. LIGHTS OUT on Trish and David and LIGHTS UP ON Alan and Karen)

ALAN. God, I hated that party.

KAREN. Okay, okay. You made that point. Let it go.

ALAN. Why? The only nice thing about this evening is coming home and being able to say what a rotten time

I had.

KAREN. Maybe if you tried talking to someone there, you would have had a nicer time.

ALAN. I did. I made several attempts. Most of those people were Hollywood executives. As soon as they found out I was a writer, they walked away.

KAREN. You didn't talk politics, did you?

ALAN. No. Not much. Maybe once or twice I mentioned that I would like to kill the President, but for the most part I was extraordinarily subdued.

KAREN. I think you chase people away on purpose and I wish you would stop it. You're getting such an anti-social reputation we hardly get invited anywhere anymore.

ALAN. Well, like they say, good fences make good neighbors.

KAREN. I have fun at parties, Alan, and I enjoy meeting and talking to everyone.

ALAN. I know. It's one of your major flaws.

KAREN. I'd like to know what my others are.

ALAN. Loyalty, devotion, pleasantness and patience. I can't relate to any of those. Anyway, can we not talk about me for awhile?

KAREN. Okay. Let's talk about Trish.

ALAN. What about her?

KAREN. We had a little chat this evening.

ALAN. Did you?

KAREN. You know we did. I caught you looking at us several times.

ALAN. Well, now and then I like to know what my wife is doing while I'm having an unbearable time.

KAREN. She asked me how our marriage was holding together?

ALAN. *(Trying not to seem too interested)* Did she?

KAREN. I thought it was a bit cheeky. Holding together? It's not exactly a vote of confidence and it's not something you just blurt out...unless you think there is something going on in the marriage...or you hope something is going on.

ALAN. Well, she may have had too much wine to drink. I brought her several glasses myself. So how did you answer her?

KAREN. I wanted to say to her that it was none of her business. But the truth is, it probably is.

ALAN. How do you figure that?

KAREN. Because she's still interested in you.

ALAN. Oh, get off it. She and David are doing quite well together.

KAREN. Maybe David is. But she's not. I had the feeling that all night she wanted to be somewhere else.

ALAN. Well, that made two of us.

KAREN. Yes. I know. And it bothered me that you two still have so much in common. I think she's very sorry she married David. I'll bet that makes you very happy to hear that, doesn't it?

ALAN. Do I suspect a hint of insecurity?

KAREN. I'd like to think of it as concern, leaning on suspicion, because I think you two are still seeing each other.

ALAN. Maybe I'll watch a little TV before I go to bed.

KAREN. You still love her, don't you Alan?

ALAN. This is a stupid conversation and I don't want to go on with it any further. Besides, there are more important things to deal with tonight. I had six pieces of pigeon and I think I'm going to throw up.

KAREN. You're avoiding the question.

ALAN. Damn it, Karen. I married you because I loved *you.* You should know me better than that. I'm too selfish a person to marry for any other reason.

KAREN. Do you love me now?

ALAN. You know I find that inquiry too incredibly dramatic

for this late in the evening.

KAREN. I love you, Alan. I have no trouble saying it. I love you. When was the last time you said that to me?

ALAN. I think there's an unwritten law that if a husband can make it through the first year of marriage, he never has to say that again.

KAREN. I don't know why I still love you Alan, but I do. You know I do.

ALAN. *(Sighs)* I know. That's what makes everything so damn difficult.

(Karen reacts. LIGHTS OUT on Alan and Karen and LIGHTS UP on David and Trish)

DAVID. Did you ever love me, Trish?

TRISH. I thought I did, David. I really thought I did.

DAVID. I remember when I asked you to marry me and you said you would. I was dancing in the street, I was so happy. But I have to admit I was also very surprised.

TRISH. Looking back, I guess I was just as surprised. My romance with Alan was going nowhere. He seemed to always be in such a state of torment. I was younger. His pain was too hard for me to understand. Then you showed up in our lives. So charming, so easy going, a friend to all, the exact opposite of Alan. You seemed so refreshing from Alan's somber world. But now when I see things for what they are, the way you treat everyone like they're your best friend when I know they're not, the way you act so interested in them when I know you aren't, that fake enthusiasm, well, the truth is, David, I admired it all at the beginning because I thought it was all so real and sincere. But now when I watch that behavior over and over again, I tear apart inside because I realize you're such a phony.

DAVID. Goddamn it, Trish. I'm in the movie business. You have to be a phony. I need to constantly exhibit friendship and confidence. It's what's called for. Would you prefer I be like Alan, the most depressed and depressing human being alive?

TRISH. At least there's an honesty there. He is what you see.

DAVID. Look, I know Alan a little better than you. Since the day I met him he has been nothing but cynical and negative. And that's exactly how you felt about him when the two of you were living together.

TRISH. Maybe that's what made him the great writer he is. He knows it's a bullshit world.

DAVID. He isn't that great. He's a movie writer. He's just lucky to have been re-written great.

TRISH. His script won you an Academy Award.

DAVID. Look, I obviously like him as a writer or I wouldn't put up with him. You're not having second thoughts about him, are you?

TRISH. We just weren't ready for each other.

DAVID. It started up again, hasn't it? Dammit, when I got involved with you, you were totally fed up with his bitching and moaning. Well, trust me, he hasn't changed. He's the same jerk he's always been.

TRISH. But he's real, don't you understand. It's him. It's no facade. No front. No appearance for appearance sake.

DAVID. What you're saying is that basically, he's not me.

TRISH. He can't deal with this bullshit life and neither can I anymore.

DAVID. Oh, please. He's just as much a part of it as anyone is. I can't believe you want to go back to that...that pretentious, smug, pompous...

TRISH. I still love him, David. And he still loves me. We both realize we made a mistake.

DAVID. And Karen? What about her? She'll be devastated.

TRISH. She's much stronger than you think. Try to understand, David. We're married to the wrong people. We're all married to the wrong people.

(LIGHTS OUT on David and Trish and LIGHTS UP on Alan and Karen)

KAREN. You're having an affair with her, aren't you?

ALAN. No.

KAREN. Don't lie. You don't have to lie.

ALAN. No. I'm not. We have lunch once in awhile, but I'm not having an affair with her.

KAREN. I think you are.

ALAN. I'm not.

(A beat)

Okay, I am.

KAREN. Oh, Alan.

ALAN. I feel awful. I really do.

KAREN. Good. You should. Does David know?

ALAN. Not yet.

KAREN. He'll be crushed. He really loves her.

ALAN. David's a movie producer. He's very use to the fact that some screenplays work out and some screenplays don't.

KAREN. I wish I could hate you, Alan.

ALAN. I wish you would.

KAREN. I knew how much you hurt when Trish and David married. I was aware of the hole it left inside you. I was hoping to be the patch that fixed it.

ALAN. I know. I know you did.

KAREN. I'll leave in the morning.

ALAN. No. No, I will.

KAREN. This is your house.

ALAN. We'll let the lawyers handle everything. For now though, I want you to stay here.

KAREN. Well, Alan, you were right about one thing tonight. It was a rotten party.

(LIGHTS OUT on Karen and Alan. LIGHTS UP and now Trish is sitting next to Alan)

ALAN. What a night. What a lousy, awful, night. What a stupid, miserable, dreadful, crappy, stinky, pukey night.

TRISH. I had a nice evening.

ALAN. It was a surprise bumping into them, wasn't it?

TRISH. I knew we would sooner or later. It's a small business, we travel in the same circles. Anyway, they seemed to be very happy.

ALAN. Why wouldn't they be happy? He's got Tom Cruise for his next movie. You weren't uncomfortable, were you?

TRISH. A bit. You?

ALAN. A bit.

TRISH. I just wish we didn't hug one another. It would have made it a lot easier if we hadn't. I could feel the insincerity. The blatant insincerity.

ALAN. I was surprised about the hugs myself. We put them both through the ringer and they greeted us like we were long lost friends. They both looked pretty good, didn't they?

TRISH. Yes, but so do we. In a way I'm glad they got together. Surprised, but glad. It helped ease the guilt.

ALAN. Well, I doubt they married out of love. I know Karen too well. She marries out of sympathy. I think it was simply a union of two damaged souls seeking refuge from the storm. Still, sometimes that kind of relationship ends up much stronger.

(A beat)

TRISH. You miss her, don't you? I saw the way you kissed her on the cheek. It said it all.

ALAN. Yes, I miss her. I never thought I would, but I do. And then seeing her again…I don't know what the hell it is with me. I want one thing one time and another thing another time, God, I'm so screwed up. How was it for you seeing David?

TRISH. It was fine. But I liked David, I never loved him. I always thought I loved you.

ALAN. Loved. That's past tense, isn't it?

TRISH. We made a mistake, didn't we Alan?

ALAN. Yeah, I guess. But then we might just be two people who will never know what they want. So, what do we do now?

TRISH. If we're smart, probably nothing.

ALAN. Yeah. That's what I think too. The good news is, this is really the kind of story I like to write. I'll bet I can sell it to David.

(Alan puts his arm around her and draws her close)

TRISH. I'll bet you could too.

(LIGHTS OUT on Alan and Trish and UP on Karen and David)

DAVID. How was it seeing him?

KAREN. Fine.

DAVID. You had no problem?

KAREN. None.

DAVID. Good.

KAREN. But you did, didn't you?

DAVID. Yes. A little bit. Don't forget, I wanted it to work between Trish and myself. Leaving was her decision.

KAREN. Well, surprisingly I felt nothing for Alan. Nothing at all. Do you want to know why?

DAVID. I do.

KAREN. Because I truly love you.

DAVID. Do you?

KAREN. I do.

DAVID. Well, that puts a new spin on everything, doesn't it?

KAREN. Yes, it does. A new spin.

DAVID. Good! Because I think...No, I know, I will eventually learn to love you.

KAREN. I hope so.

(He looks at her and kisses her)

DAVID. Karen.

KAREN. Yes.

DAVID. Thank you for marrying me.

KAREN. Don't mention it.

> *(They kiss again)*

DAVID. I wonder if…

KAREN. Yes.

DAVID. I wonder if I can get Alan to write this story.

> *(LIGHTS FADE)*

End of Act I, Scene 4

ACT II

Scene 5

THE FAILURE

TIME: *The present. Late evening.*

PLACE: *An upscale living room*

WILLIAM *and his wife,* **VICTORIA,** *both in their early fifties, sit in two winged back chairs. Victoria is engrossed in a gardening magazine as William stares into space. After a few moments he heaves a heavy sigh.*

WILLIAM. I'm a failure, aren't I?

(There is no response from Victoria, he continues)

I said, I'm a failure, aren't I?

(He looks over at Victoria. Still no response)

For the third time, I said, I'm a...

VICTORIA. *(Still not looking up)* I heard you, William. I heard you.

WILLIAM. Well, what do you think? Do you think I'm a failure?

VICTORIA. *(Finally looking up, but not at William)* Of course not. No more than most husbands.

(Back to her magazine)

WILLIAM. *(Annoyed. Looks at her)* What kind of answer is that?

VICTORIA. *(Now to William)* Well, obviously, William, living in a nice home in the suburbs, owning a large successful brokerage house and having a seven figure bank account does not exactly spell failure in any materialistic sense of the word, so I assume the only other place you'd be considering yourself a failure would be in the domestic arena. And let's face it, that's where most husbands fall down. So what's the big deal?

WILLIAM. I was referring to my inner failure, Victoria. What's inside me, which at this moment seems like a total absence of substance, meaning and importance of any kind.

VICTORIA. I see.

(She goes back to her magazine)

WILLIAM. What do you mean, you see? I'm going through an alarming awakening here. Don't you think you should show some sort of interest? Offer some sort of support, maybe some contradictory assurance, a little participation?

VICTORIA. *(Looking at him)* I had no idea you were asking for any of those things. You seemed to just be making a declaration, and for better or worse, I thought it best to go along with it, until this feeling of failure that you have hopefully passes.

WILLIAM. I don't think it's going to be that simple. I'm into some very upsetting introspection. I have come to the realization that at this juncture in my life, I'm still not a fulfilled person. I feel like I haven't lived up to my expectations.

VICTORIA. I see.

(She returns to reading her magazine)

WILLIAM. What is with this, "I see" business? God, Victoria, I'm crying out for help. The least you can do is try to calm me down, quiet my thoughts, contend that these feelings are unfounded.

VICTORIA. Well, I guess I could try. But I'd really like to finish this article I'm reading first. I'm almost done.

WILLIAM. It must be one hell of an article. What's it about?

VICTORIA. Geraniums.

WILLIAM. The flower?

VICTORIA. Yes.

WILLIAM. You find reading about a geranium more important than the turmoil and confusion I'm going through?

VICTORIA. No, William. Not more important. Just more fascinating.

(Lowers the magazine to her lap)

William, we've been married over twenty-five years and for the most part we seem to be somewhat happy. I had always hoped that would be enough. Be realistic, William. On a scale of one to ten, how satisfied with one's life does anyone need to be? I am overjoyed with a six. Please do us both a favor at this time. Don't examine your life too closely. At this point, trust me, nothing good can come from it.

WILLIAM. Victoria, right now on that scale I feel like a two. Maybe even lower. I feel so...so empty inside, so useless, so hopeless. I wonder what the age limit is on mid-life crisis.

VICTORIA. Oh, please, William. You had your mid-life crisis years ago. In fact, if you remember you had two of them.

WILLIAM. I did?

VICTORIA. Yes. The first time was when your business wasn't going too well and we couldn't meet the house payments. You were toying with a career change and you thought you'd like to be an astronaut. For weeks you walked around with a huge fish bowl over your head.

WILLIAM. Yes, that's right. Till this day I can't remember what I did with the fish. What about my second mid-life crisis?

VICTORIA. That was the time your business took an amazing upward turn and you realized you were going to be too wealthy to continue being a Democrat.

WILLIAM. Oh, yes. That was a real eye opener.

VICTORIA. Well, you got through those difficulties with flying colors and you'll get through this as well. Now, I'd really like to get back to this article.

WILLIAM. *(Disappointed by her lack of genuine concern)* About geraniums?

VICTORIA. Yes. It's really an eye opener. If you only knew what a geranium goes through in its lifetime.

WILLIAM. Oh, come on. What kind of a problem could a geranium have? It lives, it dies. A total meaningless existence if you asked me.

VICTORIA. Exactly. And the geranium has no problem with that. That's why I think you should read it. Life is not all that complicated, William. It's possible you might be placing too much importance on it.

WILLIAM. You could be right. Maybe I just have too much time on my hands.

VICTORIA. Maybe you ought to think about a hobby to dispel your thoughts. A lot of people in your predicament take up painting or writing.

WILLIAM. Writing? Yeah, that's not a bad idea. But what would I write about?

VICTORIA. Since you seem to be under stress, I would suggest something that won't take very much thinking.

WILLIAM. Yes. Like an autobiography.

VICTORIA. No. Maybe something a bit more interesting.

WILLIAM. Okay, what about that fishing trip I went on three summers ago with Brad and Howard? That seemed sort of interesting. Especially the third day out when Brad accused Howard of sleeping with his wife and pulled out a gun and shot him dead. That might make a good yarn. And then my having to help Brad hide the body and make up the story about his being swept away over a water fall. What do you think of that idea?

VICTORIA. Oh, my, would you believe I just finished a book with that exact plot. It was a fun read. But you're on the right track, so keep thinking.

WILLIAM. I can't. My head is too filled with questions that I don't have answers for. This journey of life. What was it all about? What was my contribution to it? What is my legacy? In my entire time on this planet, did I make any kind of memorable statement?

VICTORIA. Of course you did. What about at your mother's funeral when you showed up wearing her clothes? I think that was an attempt at some sort of declaration.

WILLIAM. Not really. I just over-dosed on valium and didn't know what the hell I was doing. My sister is still in the mental ward because of that. Maybe, my whole problem is that I'm simply starting to feel my own mortality. I know death is inevitable and I'm not going to beat it. Up until now I thought it couldn't happen to me. I would be an exception and go on forever. But now as I get closer to the grim reaper's appearance, I've accepted the truth. Death is indeed going to come for me and that's that. There's nothing I can do about it. Damn it, you'd really think that as one grew older the meaning of ones life would become less puzzling.

VICTORIA. William, I need to be very honest with you. At this time in my life…I can't hear this shit.

WILLIAM. No?

VICTORIA. No. You see, one of the reasons I married you, William, was because I thought you were extremely uncomplicated. I wanted to avoid headaches and uncomplicated people don't give you headaches. You came close several times, but you never did. Well, now you're giving me one and I find it very upsetting. Although I would like to be more sympathetic, more understanding, frankly I'm not prepared to make that kind of an abrupt turn in my life.

WILLIAM. Go on.

VICTORIA. I guess what I'm basically trying to say is that in order to preserve this wonderful relationship that we've enjoyed for so many years, you may need to go down other roads. Do you understand my drift?

WILLIAM. No, not really.

VICTORIA. Maybe start drinking, William. It's always helped me. I'm up to two bottles of wine a day and I've never felt better. It takes my mind off of a lot of disturbing things. In fact, I hardly ever think of the children anymore.

WILLIAM. Well, maybe it's something I'll just have to work out by myself.

VICTORIA. That's a wonderful idea. It's an excellent place to start.

(Rising)

Well, bed time. Are you coming up?

WILLIAM. Not just yet. I'd like to just sit here a little while longer and do a little more reflecting by myself.

VICTORIA. Good for you, William. Good for you. Good night, dear.

WILLIAM. Good night, Victoria. Oh, would you dim the lights a bit. I'd like to reflect in the dark. Things sometimes clear up for me better in the dark.

VICTORIA. Of course. Good night again.

WILLIAM. Yes, good night again.

(Victoria EXITS. William sits in a dim light for a few beats)

WILLIAM. *(CONTINUED)* Well, at least the marriage works.

(LIGHTS FADE TO BLACK)

THE END

PROPS/SET PIECES

ACT I

SPLITTING ISSUES
Love seat
2 side chairs
Coffee table
Small table
Dishes
2 cheese knives
4 wine glasses
1 bottle red wine
1 bottle white wine
Napkins
Plates
Cork screw
Cheese platter
Cheese *(Brie and Cheddar)*
Crackers on a dish
Bowl of onion dip
Carnations
Vase
Box of candy

DO YOU COME HERE OFTEN?
2 Chairs

PURGATORY
2 chairs
Café table
Cocktail glass

MAY I RECOMMEND THE CROW?
Chair
Café table
Menu
Restaurant table setting
Table cloth
Cloth dinner napkin

ACT II

CLEARING THE AIR
None

BINGO-BANGO
A backless bench

DINNER WITH FRIENDLY NEIGHBORS
Semi-circular restaurant booth
4 restaurant place settings
4 menus
4 glasses of water
4 napkins
Table cloth

HOLLYWOOD LOVE STORY
4 chairs or 2 small benches

THE FAILURE
2 wing back chairs
Gardening Magazine

COSTUMES

ACT I

SPLITTING ISSUES
PETE – Slacks, shirt, watch
GWEN – Skirt, blouse
LARRY – Slacks, corduroy jacket, sport shirt
MARCIE – Skirt, expensive sweater set, pearl necklace

DO YOU COME HERE OFTEN?
BOB – Loud sport coat, colored shirt, colored tie
NAN – Flashy out-of-place party dress

PURGATORY
JACK – Tennis outfit, shirt, shorts, shoes
RICHARD – Sport coat, slacks, shirt

MAY I RECOMMEND THE CROW?
JOYCE – Elegant dress
CHARLES – Waiter's tuxedo, shirt, bowtie

ACT II

CLEARING THE AIR
CLARK – Jacket, pants, shirt, tie
JILL – Skirt, blouse
EMMA – Dress
HARRISON – Sport coat, slacks, turtleneck sweater

BINGO-BANGO
ROSALIND – Skirt, sweater
FRED – Slacks, shirt
ZOE – Slacks, sweater
IAN – Slacks, shirt

DINNER WITH FRIENDLY NEIGHBORS
DONNA – Slacks, sweater
NICK – Slacks, shirt
IRENE – Conservative suit
WAYNE – Sport coat, slacks, shirt

HOLLYWOOD LOVE STORY
ALAN – Sport coat, turtleneck, slacks
KAREN – Skirt, blouse
DAVID – Suit, tie
TRISH – Pant suit

<u>**THE FAILURE**</u>
WILLIAM – Sport shirt, slacks
VICTORIA – Everyday dress

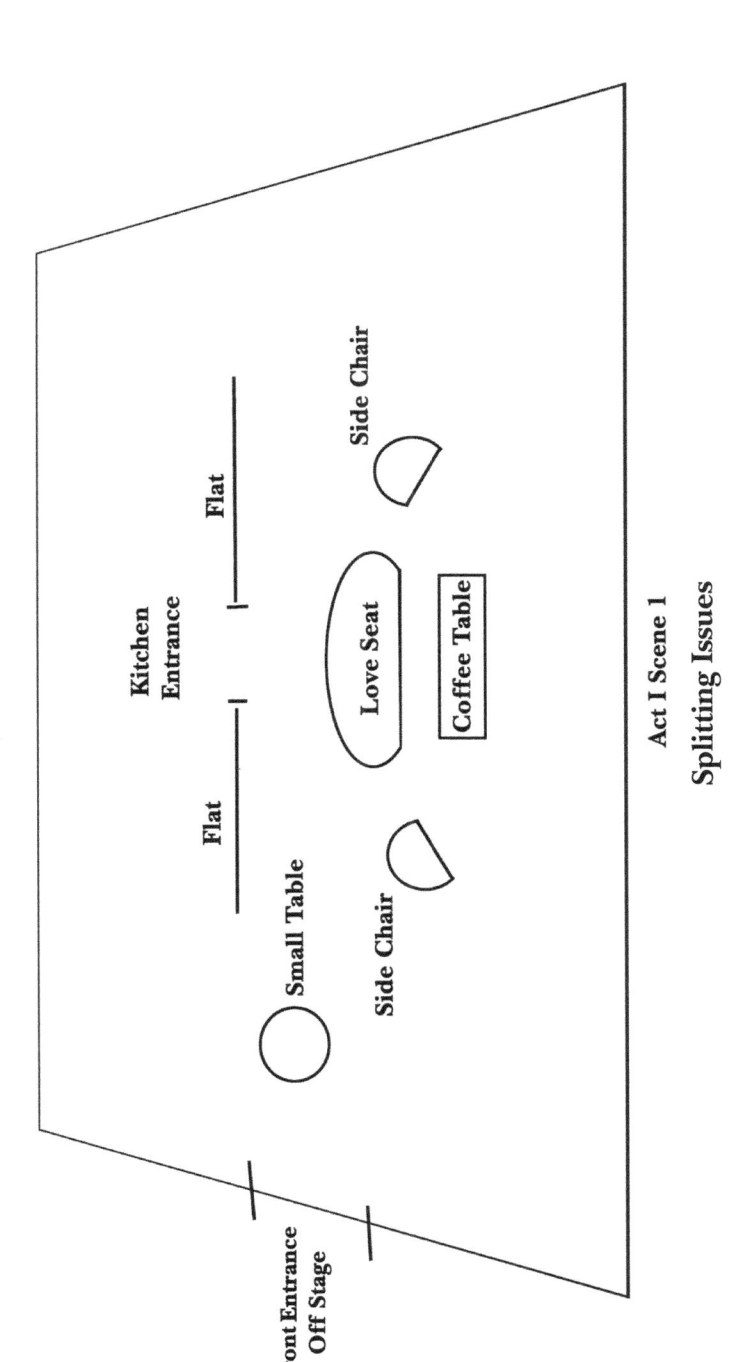

Front Entrance
Off Stage

Small Table

Side Chair

Flat

Kitchen
Entrance

Flat

Love Seat

Coffee Table

Side Chair

Act I Scene 1
Splitting Issues

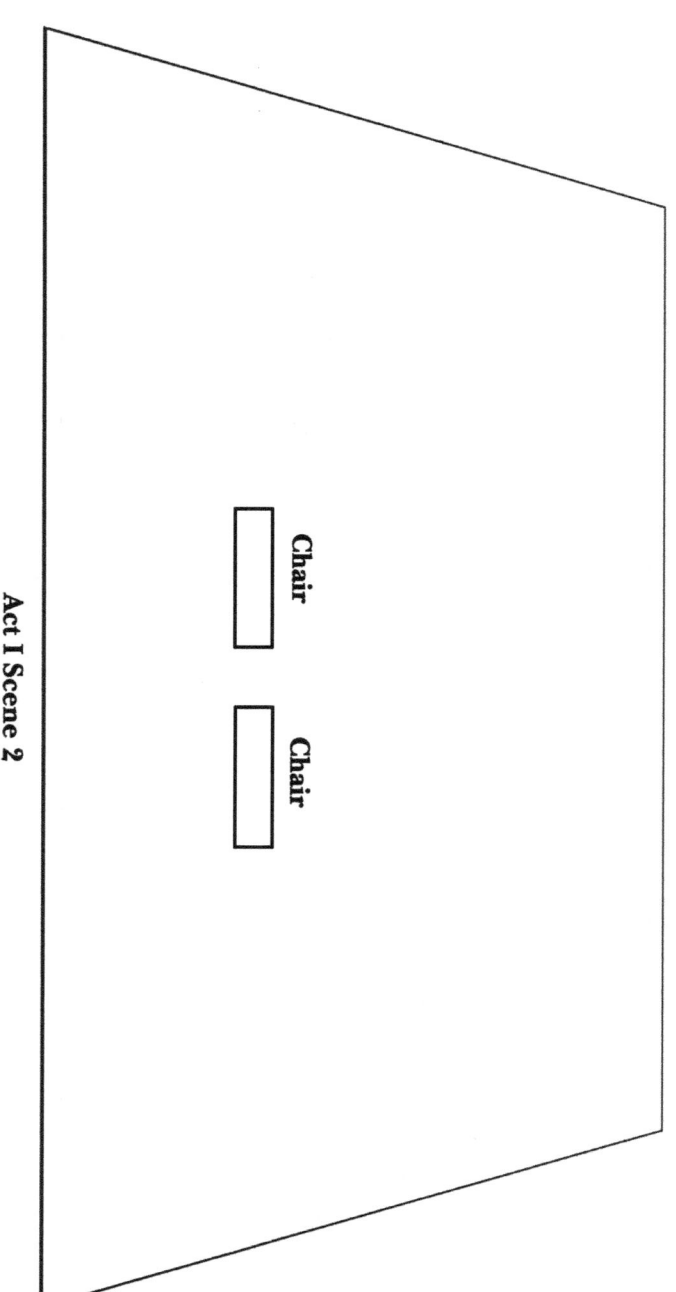

Act I Scene 2
Do You Come Here Often?

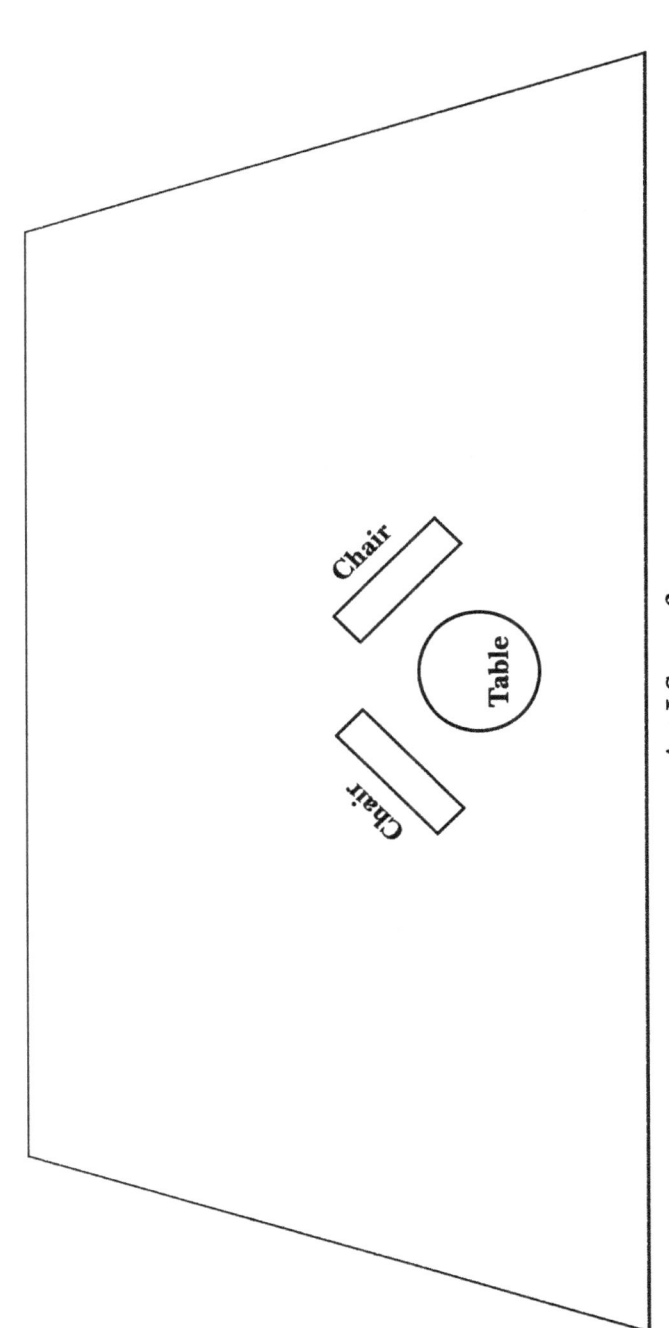

Act I Scene 3

Purgatory

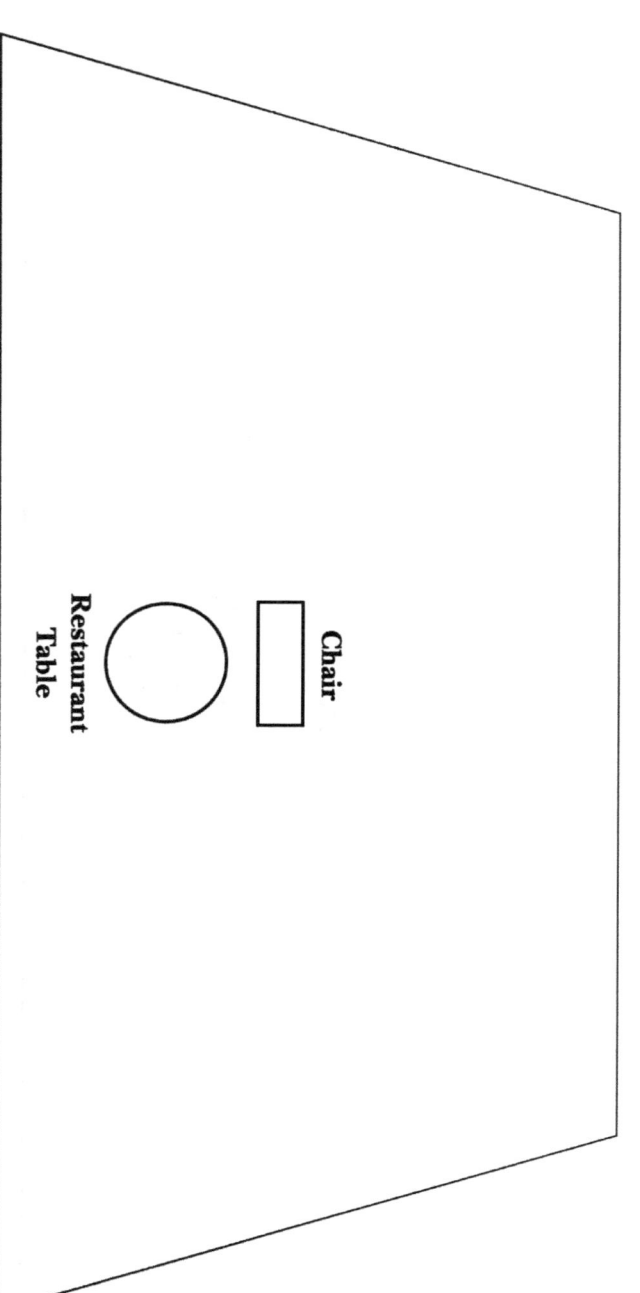

Act I Scene 4

May I Recommend The Crow?

Chair

Restaurant
Table

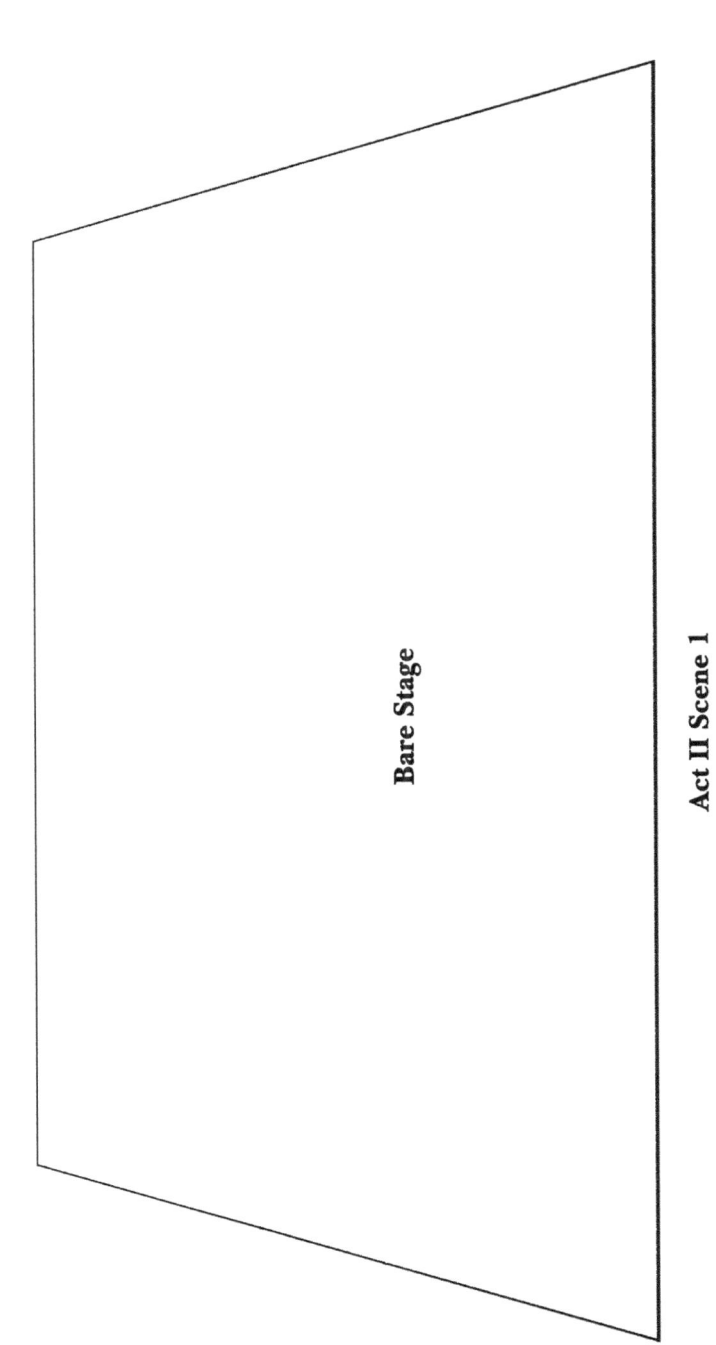

Bare Stage

Act II Scene 1
Clearing the Air

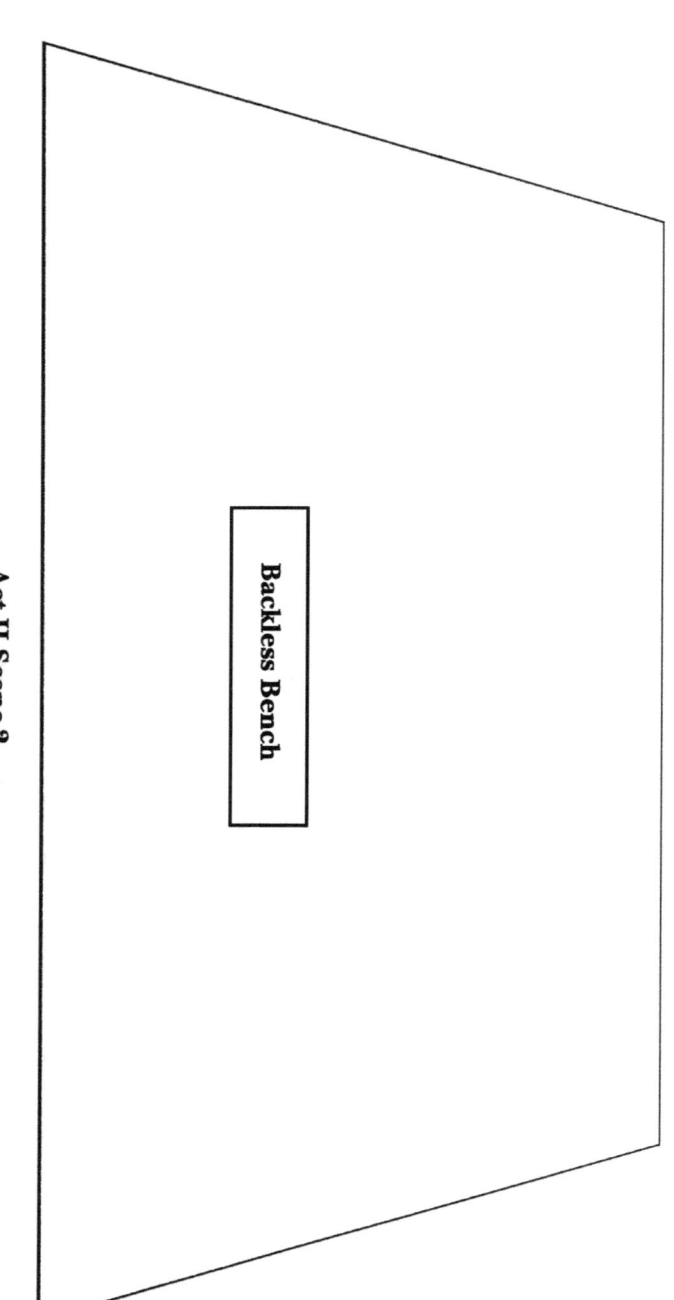

Backless Bench

Act II Scene 2
Bingo-Bango

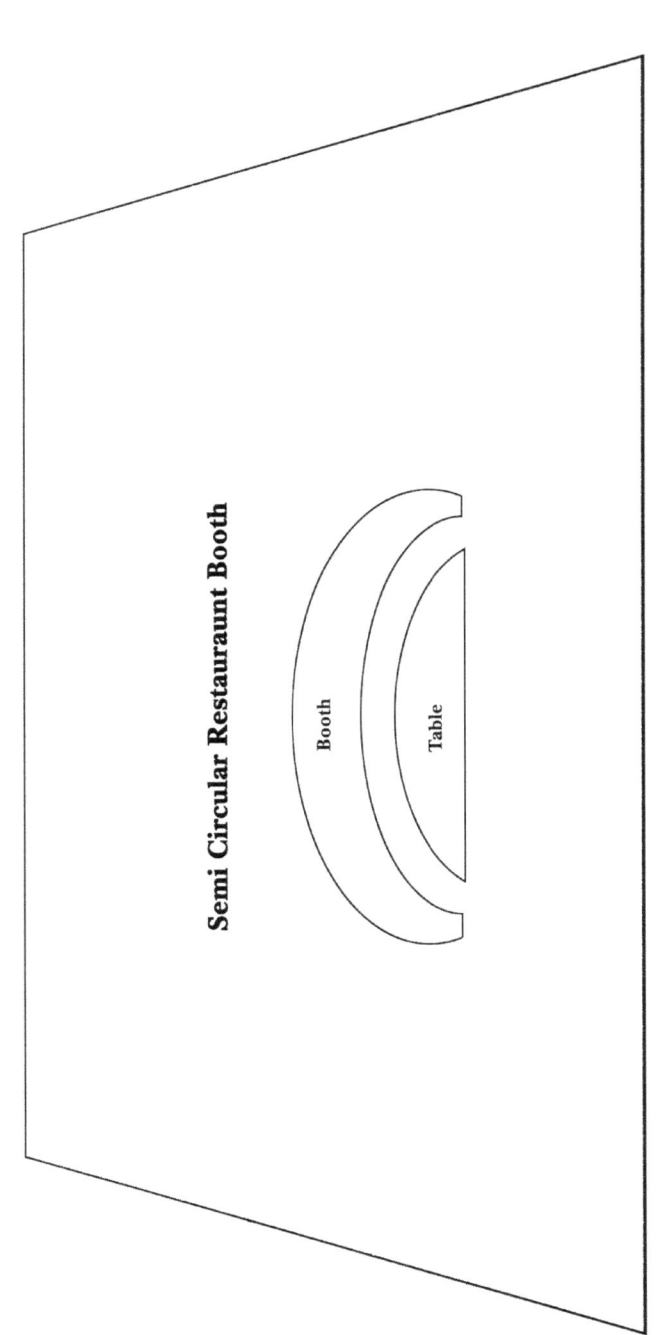

Semi Circular Restauraunt Booth

Booth

Table

Act II Scene 3

Dinner with Friendly Neighbors

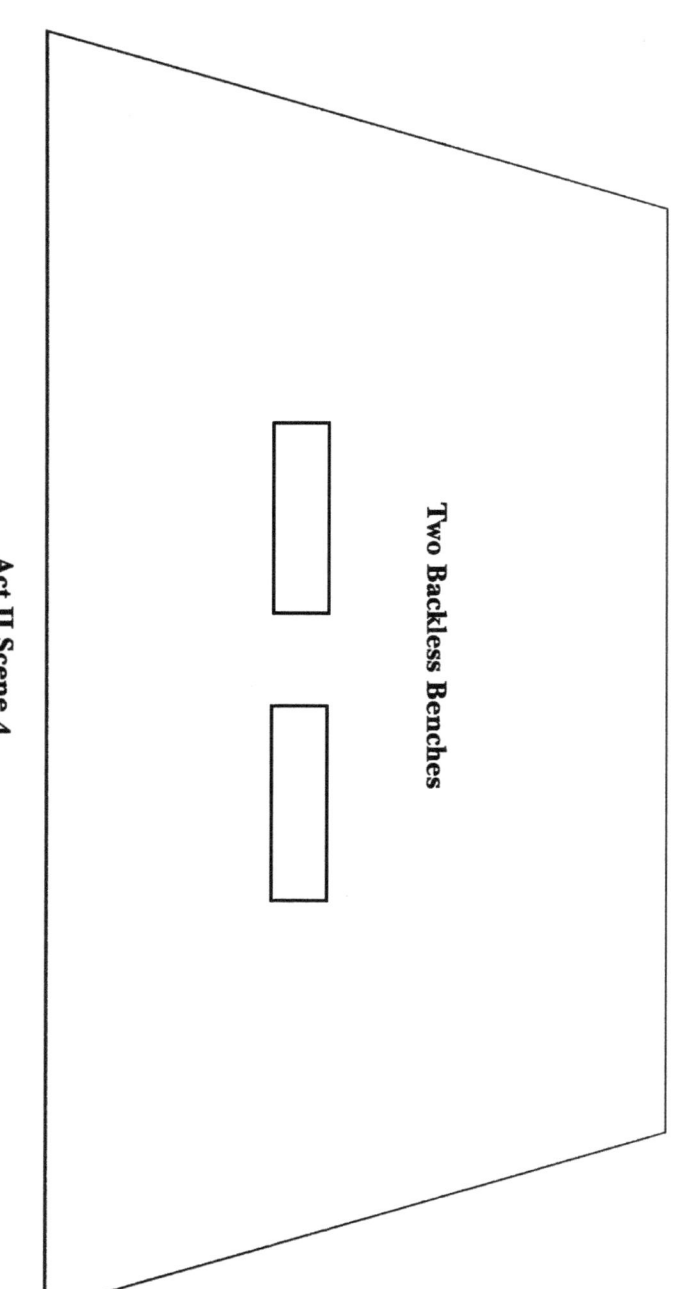

Two Backless Benches

Act II Scene 4
Hollywood Love Story

Two Wing Back Chairs

Act II Scene 5
The Failure

Also by
Sam Bobrick...

Annoyance
Are You Sure?
Baggage
The Crazy Time
Death in England
Flemming (An American Thriller)
Getting Sara Married
Hamlet II (Better Than the Original)
Last Chance Romance
Murder at the Howard Johnson's
New York Water
No Hard Feelings
Norman, Is That You?
The Outrageous Adventures of
Sheldon and Mrs. Levine
Passengers
Remember Me?
The Stanway Case
Wally's Cafe
Weekend Comedy

Please visit our website **samuelfrench.com** for complete
descriptions and licensing information

OTHER TITLES AVAILABLE FROM SAMUEL FRENCH

MAURITIUS
Theresa Rebeck

Comedy / 3m, 2f / Interior

Stamp collecting is far more risky than you think. After their mother's death, two estranged half-sisters discover a book of rare stamps that may include the crown jewel for collectors. One sister tries to collect on the windfall, while the other resists for sentimental reasons. In this gripping tale, a seemingly simple sale becomes dangerous when three seedy, high-stakes collectors enter the sisters' world, willing to do anything to claim the rare find as their own.

"(Theresa Rebeck's) belated Broadway bow, the only original play by a woman to have its debut on Broadway this fall."
- Robert Simonson, *New York Times*

"*Mauritius* caters efficiently to a hunger that Broadway hasn't been gratifying in recent years. That's the corkscrew-twist drama of suspense… she has strewn her script with a multitude of mysteries."
- Ben Brantley, *New York Times*

"Theresa Rebeck is a slick playwright… Her scenes have a crisp shape, her dialogue pops, her characters swagger through an array of showy emotion, and she knows how to give a plot a cunning twist."
- John Lahr, *The New Yorker*